CATHERINE GRANGER e̶ ̶ ̶ ̶ ̶ ̶ ̶ number of doubts as she took a last look around the flat that had been home to her and the boys for the past three and a half years. That was the last time any of them had seen their father, for George Granger had always spent a great deal of time abroad; no matter what crises arose in the family, he was invariably absent when they arose.

Although he had always professed to be a staunch patriot, he had lived almost all his adult life overseas, in much warmer climes than England – and always unencumbered by the family he professed to love so much and with whom he spent so little time.

He had been somewhere in eastern Europe at the time when Catherine's mother died, ten years ago, and he had returned only briefly to attend to matters that Catherine was, at that time, too young to cope with. But he had disappeared again very soon afterwards, leaving eleven-year-old Catherine in a boarding school which she hated.

Only two years after that he had returned to England again with a young Greek wife. Maria Granger was a gentle, kind creature, and having a stepmother meant that Catherine could leave the school she hated so much and return to her former type of education. Maria had taken Catherine under her wing and the two of them had been company for one another during George Granger's long absences.

Maria spoke quite good English, so there was no language problem, but it did not take Catherine long to realize that Maria would have been much better off with her own family in Greece than in a strange country where she knew no one and with her husband away for so long at a time. For Maria saw very little more of her husband than his first wife had.

During the five and a half years of their marriage she had given George Granger two little sons, and Catherine was as adoring a stepsister as it was possible to find. She had been heartbroken when Maria died. giving birth to the younger boy, and it was certain that she missed her young stepmother a good deal more than her father did.

Once again George Granger came home to bury his wife, consoled his daughter in his own rather off-hand fashion and then left again after a few weeks. He had been even less concerned this time about leaving Catherine, for she was now eighteen years old and both willing and able to take care of the two tiny boys.

Their father had seen them installed in an expensively comfortable flat, complete with an attendant housekeeper, and departed again for the island of Dakolis. Dakolis was the home of his second wife and he had acquired an interest in the shipping and export company belonging to Maria's family.

Neither Catherine nor his two infant sons had seen anything more of him after that, which was no real surprise to Catherine, although she had rather ex-

pected him to take more interest in his sons. It was three weeks ago that a cablegram had arrived one morning, announcing that George Granger had been drowned in a boating accident while sailing off the Greek coast. The cablegram was signed Stefan Medopolis.

It would have been hypocritical of Catherine to mourn her father, for she had seen so little of him during his lifetime that he was virtually a stranger, and his two sons did not even know what he looked like.

There had been no question of Catherine attending the funeral either, because it had taken place very soon after his death and it had simply not been possible to arrange for someone to take care of the two little boys, and to organize her own flight out to Greece, in the time.

A short and very formal letter had explained the reasons for such haste in having the funeral within days, and had expressed brief and formal condolence in her loss, for the sender must have been fully aware of George Granger's shortcomings as a parent. The letter too had been signed by Stefan Medopolis.

He was Maria's eldest brother, that much Catherine knew, although Maria had spoken surprisingly little about her home, perhaps because she missed it so much. Catherine also knew, via a rare letter from her father shortly after Maria's death, that their uncle was anxious to take the two little boys into his care. He was the head of his family, and he saw it as his duty to care for his sister's orphaned sons.

7

George Granger had declined at the time, possibly because it would have meant being in too close proximity to his responsibilities, and Catherine had been vastly relieved not to lose her two little charges.

Now, it seemed, he had had second thoughts about leaving his two sons in the sole care of their half-sister. The letter she held in her hands, and which she had just read for the hundredth time, was from Stefan Medopolis's lawyer, and informed her that the boys' father had declared himself in favour of their uncle taking over guardianship of them.

It had come as a distinct shock to Catherine to learn so suddenly that the two little half-brothers she had cared for ever since their mother's death three and a half years before were to be taken away from her, and she could not yet reconcile herself to the fact.

They were a close little group, and Catherine had not yet plucked up sufficient courage to tell the boys that they were soon to go and live in a foreign country with an uncle they had never seen, and would perhaps never see her again. She could scarcely bear to face the fact herself, and still could not quite believe it.

Catherine was to travel with them as far as Nicosia, and see them safely handed over to their uncle, and she would have to think of some way of breaking it to them on the journey out there. It would be particularly difficult to make little Paul understand, for he would be heartbroken when he realized that he would never see his beloved 'Catine' again.

Catherine was the only mother he had ever known, and at only three and a half he was still very de-

pendent on her. Alex, at five, was hardly more than a baby either, and she dared not think what would happen when they learned that she would be going back to England without them, leaving them surrounded by strangers.

She had paid off Mrs. Harrison, the housekeeper, and the kindly woman had been touched enough by the prospect before them to wipe away a tear when she said good-bye to the two little boys. She had looked at Catherine and shaken her head sadly, thinking that she looked scarcely more than a child herself.

The boys were, at the moment, highly excited by it all, and they chattered happily amid the mound of luggage, while Catherine sat on one of the armchairs, waiting for their transport to arrive. Her small face had a despondent look, although she was doing her best not to let the boys know how she felt.

She had a fragile, pale look that was deceptive, with deep, copper-coloured hair and huge green eyes, a small nose that was inclined to tilt at the end and a wide, soft mouth that was usually smiling. A girl to attract a second look and more, as she often did, although many would-be suitors had been discouraged by her devotion to her two little brothers.

It was a warm day and the pale green dress she wore gave her a cool, little-girl look that was infinitely appealing. Her sigh went unnoticed in the eager chatter of the two little boys, and she managed a smile when Paul, the younger one, came and leaned against her knee, his enormous dark eyes sparkling mischief.

He was so tiny and so much like his mother that

9

Catherine had at least the consolation of knowing that, physically anyway, he should have no difficulty in fitting into the Greek part of his family. Alexander was only a little less dark, and he too had those huge dark eyes that could surely melt an iceberg. It was to be hoped that their new guardian was less unbending than his letters gave the impression of.

She thought for a moment that Paul was about to start asking questions again, and she told herself that she was a coward for being glad to hear the door bell announce the arrival of their transport. There was so little time left now, but somewhere deep inside her she knew that she was hoping for a last-minute miracle. Something that would change Stefan Medopolis's mind about taking them, and leave them still in her care.

It seemed incredible that it was barely five hours since they had left Heathrow, and here they were already skimming down on to the runway at Nicosia airport. A different country, a different world, and all so heart-stoppingly lovely that Catherine felt her spirits lift, despite the reason for her journey.

She had promised herself a holiday before she went back. Perhaps an excuse to stay just a little longer within reasonable distance of the boys before she flew away altogether. It was an optimistic, perhaps a silly thing to do in the circumstances, but when she saw how beautiful Cyprus was, she made up her mind.

It was a soft, warm evening, with a sun more flamboyantly brilliant than any she had ever seen before, and she would love to have gone exploring there and then, taking the boys with her, of course, although they were now getting a little sleepy and tired after their journey and less chattily excited.

'Miss Granger?'

The question was soft-voiced, but it brought Catherine round swiftly to face the questioner, her hands instinctively gathering the two little boys close to her. She nodded, her green eyes dark and wary of the young man who smiled at her.

He was tall and very dark, and he reminded her of Maria so that she already guessed his identity before he announced it, extending a hand to take hers. 'I am Gregori Medopolis,' he said, and Catherine blinked for a moment, briefly thrown off balance by the unexpected.

She knew there was more than one brother, of course, but somehow she had expected Stefan Medopolis to meet them. This was obviously one of his brothers. One thing at least was a relief – the man before her was very good-looking and he was also smiling a welcome, which was something she had not really expected from the tone of the letters she had received.

'I'm very glad to meet you, Mr. Medopolis.' She looked down at Alex and Paul, gazing up at the stranger with a dark, uncertain look in their eyes, holding tightly to Catherine's hands. 'This is Alexander and Paul. Boys, this is your uncle.'

Gregori Medopolis bent his tall body in half to bring himself nearer their height, and he took each solemnly presented small hand in his for a moment, retaining his hold on Paul's because his bottom lip was quivering warningly and his eyes looked heavily tired. 'You will like it here,' he promised. 'I too have little children, but—' broad expressive shoulders shrugged resignation, 'they are both girls. There is much for children to do, many places to go, you will enjoy it.'

'Catine too?' Paul asked – inevitably, Catherine recognized, and her heart sank when Gregori Medopolis caught her eye for a moment and raised one brow.

'They're not used to being – alone,' Catherine explained quietly, feeling that she would make a fool of herself and cry if she had to stand here and answer questions, right here and now.

'Ah, I see!'

The dark eyes, so like Maria's and the boys', held sympathy, and he nodded his head. It was all going to be so much harder than she had expected, and Catherine wished she could have made the break in England, and not come out here with them. The longer she left it, the harder it became to explain to them.

'I – I just haven't had the chance—' she began, and shook her head, but Gregori Medopolis took her arm in a kindly reassuring gesture that was almost her undoing.

'It will be easier after a few more days, perhaps,' he said. 'I am to fly you to Dakolis right now, if you will come with me.'

One hand indicated a large, shiny private plane at the side of the airfield, and for a moment Catherine's spirits rose again, then she shook her head, biting her lip as she foresaw even greater difficulties if she stayed with them, even for one night, in their new home.

'I – I can't come with you,' she said, her eyes bright with unshed tears, and her fingers curled tightly round the two little hands that would surely refuse to loose hers however much she tried to free herself. 'It wasn't – I wasn't supposed to come too, I mean—'

Again that kindly hand reassured her and Gregori Medopolis smiled slowly. 'It is all arranged, Miss Granger,' he said quietly. 'You are to stay at the house until the little ones have – settled in. Stefan has said so.'

Stefan has said so! That sounded more like the man who had written her those stiffly formal letters, and she instinctively resented the suggestion of authority. There had been no one to wield authority over her for most of her life, and Catherine had managed very well without a man to organize her plans for her. She had little liking for the idea of Stefan Medopolis deciding that she would stay with the boys until they had settled in, although it was the obvious thing for her to do.

'It's – it's very kind of Mr. Medopolis,' she said, husky-voiced with the emotion that threatened to choke her. 'I – I didn't anticipate coming with them, I mean—' She bit her lip and saw again the warm glint of compassion in Gregori Medopolis's eyes.

'It is understood that it would be hard,' he said quietly. 'That is why Stefan thought—' Broad elegant shoulders shrugged meaningly. 'He is not such a hard man, Miss Granger, if he does give the impression at times. I hope you will come with us.'

Catherine looked down at Paul and Alex, two pairs

of big, dark eyes that were now not only anxious but almost tearful, as if they realized what was going on, and their fingers in hers clung more tightly. 'Thank you,' she whispered, and Gregori Medopolis nodded and smiled his satisfaction.

Gregori Medopolis was an expert pilot, and the boys found renewed interest in being flown in such a light plane. They had been thrilled by the big aircraft they had arrived in, but this was different. They could see so much more, and they pressed their noses to the windows as the machine skimmed away from Nicosia and out over the sea.

The sky was a brilliant gold, much more evident still this high up, and little clouds streaked the vast expanse like crushed gold silk above a sea that looked almost violet in the light of dusk. A sea as calm and smooth as a great amethyst, glittering with gold lights as the sun caught its gentle swell.

'It's beautiful,' Catherine said softly, half to herself, and Gregori Medopolis turned his head and smiled at her.

'You have never been to Greece before, Miss Granger?' he asked.

'Never.' Catherine pulled a wry face. 'I've never been anywhere very much, I'm afraid. My father was the traveller in the family, the rest of us stayed home.'

The dark eyes were shrewd and inquiring now, and Catherine was aware that to the Greeks, to whom a close family circle was traditional, her father's way of life must have been quite incomprehensible. 'You did not know your father very well?' he said, and Catherine shook her head.

'Not very well,' she admitted. 'I saw very little of him.' She glanced over her shoulder at the two little boys with their faces pressed to the windows of the plane. 'Paul hasn't seen his father since he was a few weeks old.'

'Such a pity!' The handsome dark head shook regretfully, as if he could not imagine a man willingly being parted from his children, and especially from two such fine young sons. 'A man should see his children, should see them grow, be proud of them. Your father missed so much, Miss Granger.'

'I think so,' Catherine agreed quietly. 'But—' she shrugged, 'it was the way he wanted it, I suppose.'

'They are two fine boys.' He sounded almost envious, as he too cast a brief glance over his shoulder at Paul and Alex, and Catherine thought she followed his train of thought. He had made that remark about his own family consisting of two girls, and it was obvious that he envied his late brother-in-law his sons.

'You said you have a family, Mr. Medopolis?' she asked, and he nodded.

'Two daughters,' he said. 'Alas, no son yet.'

It was a rather outmoded way of thinking, to Catherine's mind, the desire to have sons. Rather unfair and old-fashioned and, being Catherine, she was prepared to say as much, even on such short acquaintance as she had with Gregori Medopolis.

'Does it really matter if they're boys or girls?' she

15

asked. 'They're all in as much need of love, aren't they?'

For a moment the man's dark eyes turned on her curiously, then he smiled. 'You do not have the outlook that we do, Miss Granger,' he told her quietly. 'We still look upon sons as a matter for pride, although we love our daughters too, as my sister will have told you.'

Catherine shook her head slowly, her eyes distant for a moment. 'I liked Maria,' she said simply, and Gregori Medopolis looked momentarily sad.

'We loved her,' he said. 'That is why Stefan wants to have her sons.'

It was still duskily light when Gregori Medopolis landed the small aircraft skilfully and helped two sleepy little boys from their seats, lending a hand to Catherine with a delightfully old-world gallantry that pleased her.

'It is only a short drive from here to the house,' he told her, carrying Paul in his arms as he strode across the patch of green field that served as a landing field. 'These young men will soon be fast asleep in their beds.'

Catherine herself felt as if she had never been further from sleep, although she should have been at least bodily tired after the day they had had. Instead she felt as excited as a schoolgirl, and held Alex's hand tightly as they followed his uncle to the car.

A vast shiny monster that Catherine was surprised to find he drove himself. Gregori Medopolis, it seemed, was a man of independence, and needed neither

16

chauffeur nor pilot to get him from one place to another.

He sat little Paul gently in the back seat, and helped Alex in alongside him, smiling at their sleepy faces, and shaking his head. 'They are both so much like Maria,' he said softly. 'It is almost unbelievable, we were afraid—' His voice trailed off and he glanced at Catherine apologetically as he slid into the seat beside her.

'That they would look like my father?' she suggested softly, and smiled. 'It's all right, Mr. Medopolis, I'm glad they look more Greek than English, in the circumstances, since they're going to *be* Greek.'

'I meant no offence,' he apologized, and Catherine smiled, guessing that the men of the Medopolis family did not very often apologize for anything they said or did. Despite his charm and impeccable manners, there was a hint of ruthlessness in Gregori Medopolis that made her fear the same quality in his older brother, and without the charm.

They were a very wealthy family, the island of Dakolis belonged to them, as did another, smaller island further around the coast, and their shipping interests were vast and profitable. If Stefan Medopolis was the head of such a huge and complex empire it was unlikely that he would be any less self-possessed or ruthless than his brother, and much more likely to be more so, especially judging by those brief communications she had had from him.

The road they followed from the airfield was as twisting and undulating as a switchback, but the views it gave of the sea and the shoreline were breathtaking, even in this variable and uncertain light.

It was a rocky shoreline; almost like a fortress, passed uneasily through Catherine's mind as she looked at the high rugged faces of rock, but then there were little sandy coves that softened the overall effect of the rocky outline, and the sea rolled in like a ruffle of soft creamy lace down there on the sand.

There were so many different kinds of vegetation that she made no attempt to identify them all, although she could recognize palms, orange and lemon trees, hibiscus and jasmine, even in the fading light, and the overwhelming scent of them all was heady enough to make her forget, however briefly, the reason she was there.

'It's all so beautiful,' she breathed as they ran down yet another hill and twisted round another bend in the winding road. 'It's – it's sort of – unreal, somehow!'

'You will like it here,' Gregori told her seriously, and Catherine looked at him swiftly, suspicious, for no good reason that she could think of.

'I'm sure I would, if I was staying,' she replied, quietly enough for the two half-asleep little boys in the back of the car not to overhear.

'But you will be for – for a while anyway,' Gregori told her, equally quiet, and for the same reason, no doubt.

'Mr. Medopolis—' Catherine began, and was silenced before she could say more, by a raised hand that somehow had an imperious look.

'We are here,' Gregori said quietly. 'I would rather you made your objections to Stefan, Miss Granger. He is the head of the household and as such he will make his wishes known to you.'

His wishes! Catherine was already bridling with indignation when they turned another corner and ran between two tall fluted columns, half hidden by dark, plume-like cypress trees. The glimpses of the house she caught through the thick surrounding trees made her heart skip with some emotion she could not quite recognize, but Catherine thought she had never seen anything quite so beautiful.

The house was built on the narrowest tip of the island and so had the ocean on both sides of it within sight of its windows. Vast sweeping gardens, rich and luxuriant with a host of flowers and trees, half of which she did not know, ran almost down to the sea on three sides with a fringe of sandy shore fluttering round to their feet.

It was huge and breathtaking and Catherine had never seen anything remotely like it before. She looked at it all with wide, hardly believing eyes as they drove up to the house, where Gregori braked the car and got out, coming round with those swift, easy strides to assist her to alight. His manners, as always, were impeccable.

If the outside of the house had been impressive, the inside was even more so, and Catherine began to feel so much out of her depth that she wished she had not consented to come, even if it did mean her being with the boys for a little longer.

A huge airy hall, with slim columns and exquisitely tiled floor, reminded her of a Greek temple rather than a home, and her heart turned cold in her when she imagined the effect it would have on Paul and Alex, used to the rather tight confines of a London flat, however luxurious it might have been.

They walked across the impressive hall with her now, one small hand clasped tightly in each of hers, their eyes heavy with sleep and Paul inclined to be tearful, his bottom lip quivering at the strange surroundings. Despite his anxiety to hand them over to his brother, however, Gregori spared time and sympathy for the tired little boy. He bent and stroked Paul's cheek with one long finger, his dark eyes gleaming gently at the baby face, so woebegone in his strange surroundings. 'It will not be long until you are at home here, little one,' he said softly. 'But all you want at this moment is to sleep, huh?'

'Tired,' Paul agreed, and turned and buried his face against Catherine's skirt. 'Go home.'

'Darling!' She bent and lifted him into her arms, her own eyes misting when she saw the familiar droop to his mouth and the despondent little smile he gave her. 'It – it'll be like home here soon, you'll see.' She hugged him close and he laid his head on her shoulder, already half asleep, she guessed, and wished that their host would put in an appearance before he went right off. She did not look her best with one little boy nearly asleep on her shoulder and the other clinging to her skirt, his dark eyes wide and questioning and determined not to cry too.

Her prayer was answered almost at once, when one of the doors leading off the huge hall opened suddenly and a man came out, pausing briefly in his stride when he saw them, a strange, stunned look on his face which vanished almost at once before a firm, arrogant expression that made Catherine's heart sink. This *must* be Stefan Medopolis – he could quite easily have sent that stiffly formal letter that still sat in her handbag.

'Miss Granger?' He extended a hand as he approached, but there was no smile of welcome such as his brother had given her at the airport. His features were less good-looking too, and he was older than she had anticipated, in his late thirties, she guessed.

Also there was something vaguely familiar about him, although she could not for the life of her think why there should be. It was surely improbable that she had met Stefan Medopolis before, and if she had she would certainly not have forgotten him. She remembered too that Maria had told her there were two daughters between Stefan and Gregori, herself and an older sister who had died very young. The Medopolis daughters, it seemed, were short-lived.

Stefan Medopolis was taller than Gregori too, with wide shoulders and a physique that would have suited an athlete rather than a wealthy business man. There was a hawk-like quality about his features, less classically Greek than his brother's, and somehow more striking. Black-haired and black-eyed, he had an uncompromising look that did nothing to convince Catherine that he was a suitable guardian for her two little half-brothers.

The dark face had a lean hardness that did not soften, as his brother's had done, when he looked down

21

at the two little boys. 'The children must be put to bed at once,' he decided in a cool firm voice, after having exchanged the very briefest of formal greetings, and as if on cue, a dark-faced woman emerged from some hidden door in the nether regions of the house.

'Oh, but I always—' Catherine began, then swallowed the rest of the words when a large hand waved her to silence. It angered her that she obeyed its silent instruction, but there had seemed no alternative.

Alex, meanwhile, was looking at the woman in dazed horror, then he too hid his face against Catherine's skirt, his hands clutching tightly – Paul was already fast asleep, his head heavy on her shoulder. 'I'd better go with them,' Catherine said, determined this time not to be silenced, but she felt as if she was suggesting something quite outrageous by wanting to do what seemed to her to be the obvious best for all concerned. 'I always see them into bed.'

'It will not be necessary,' Stefan Medopolis told her adamantly. 'Casia is perfectly capable of putting two small boys to bed, she has had a great deal of practice.'

The woman was perhaps less formidable than she had first appeared, and her black eyes looked at Catherine with a warm glint of understanding, then she bent and touched Alex lightly on his arm and murmured something softly in her own tongue.

The novelty of the strange tongue was unusual enough to bring Alex round to face her for a moment, his huge eyes curious while he still clung to Catherine's skirt. Again the woman spoke softly in Greek, and after

22

a moment Alex looked up at Catherine and shook his head.

'I – I don't want to go,' he said, and his lips quivered warningly. 'You come too, Catine.'

Catherine looked up hastily at the set stern face of Stefan Medopolis, wondering if he intended to start his duties as guardian right here and now, or if he would allow her to break them gradually into a new routine. There was a hint of impatience in the black eyes and a firm set to his straight mouth that gave her little hope, but Catherine widened her own eyes appealingly.

'It surely wouldn't hurt,' she ventured. 'Just this once, Mr. Medopolis.'

'There is very little time before dinner. Miss Granger,' he informed her shortly. 'And you will doubtless wish to bath and change before then. Let Casia take them!'

With Alex's fingers gripping her hard and Paul completely limp on her shoulder she stood for a moment undecided. She no longer had control of the boys, it was true, Stefan Medopolis was now their guardian, but surely after the long and tiring day they had had it would not hurt just for once to let her see them into bed as she always did.

'Please,' she pleaded, some instinct telling her that appeal would be more successful than anger in this instance. 'I won't be long and – and it *is* for the best.'

He did not like her pleading with him, she could see that, and she saw the look of wonderment on the face of the woman Casia at her temerity in even attempting to change his mind. Such a thing was probably un-

23

heard-of, she guessed, and was more than ever surprised, therefore, when she realized that he had nodded his head, briefly and jerkily.

'Very well,' he told her, coldly disapproving. 'Since it is their first night here, and they are possibly overtired, you may go with Casia, but I shall be obliged if you will spend as little time as possible over it, Miss Granger. There is much to discuss after we have had dinner.'

He turned on his heel without further ado and strode off back the way he had come, obviously disliking his own decision to yield, while Catherine watched him for a moment with that faint flick of recognition again. It simply wasn't possible that she had met him before and forgotten him, and yet he had a strangely familiar look.

Gregori's hand on her arm recalled her gently, and he smiled at her encouragingly. 'We will meet again at dinner,' he said quietly. A brief squeeze of her fingers and he followed his brother across the hall. The expression on Casia's face gave Catherine a certain amount of satisfaction, for it was obvious that she did not quite believe she had seen her employer outfaced.

Catherine was almost smiling as she walked across the vast hall behind Casia, carrying Paul, and with Alex clinging on tightly to her still. Round one had gone to her, she thought, and that could surely be no mean achievement with a man of Stefan Medopolis's character.

24

CHAPTER TWO

IT was incredible how luxurious everything was, even to Catherine, who was used to living well. The wealth of the Medopolis family was way beyond anything her own father had known and they seemed to indulge in every luxury that their wealth could provide. Even the boys had their own suite of rooms, and it was the new-ness and excitement of it all that had made them less concerned about not being in familiar surroundings, so that they were not as upset as Catherine had antici-pated.

A smiling dark-eyed young maid had shown her to her own room and she had spent precious time looking around her as she bathed and changed. No matter if Stefan Medopolis had more or less instructed her to hurry, she had to take time to touch and admire the lovely marble bathroom and toiletries, and the silks and velvets that gave her bedroom a rich oriental look.

Her luggage, she discovered, had already been brought to her room and unpacked, although her rather sparse holiday wardrobe looked quite lost in the cavernous cupboards that provided for a much more extravagant choice than she possessed. She decided on a soft yellow dress in floaty voile, with wide sleeves and a low scoop neckline that showed the creamy skin of her throat and neck and quite a bit of her shoulders as well.

It was when she left her room at last and started downstairs again that she began to feel quite sickeningly nervous. She had no idea how many there were in the Medopolis household, or even if there were guests, and she fervently wished she had someone to hold her hand, even metaphorically.

The staircase was so wide and ornate, rich in marble and gold, that she felt as if she was making a stage entrance, and the huge, temple-like hall below was silent and deserted, although she could hear the murmur of voices somewhere. What she would do when she got to the bottom she had no idea, and her legs felt suddenly weak and trembly as she trod carefully.

Her red hair gleamed like copper under the lights that now illuminated the hall, and her green eyes had a wide, uncertain look between their thick brown lashes. Also she could not imagine why she felt so much as if she had done all this before. Walked down these impressive stairs and—

'Chero poli!'

The voice was deep and soft, and it cut across her thoughts so that she turned her head swiftly and rather nervously. She had noticed no one about until he spoke and she wondered where he had come from. He was quite young, no more than a year or two more than her own twenty-one years, she thought, and from his looks he was very evidently one of the Medopolis family. Very probably the third brother, although he was so much younger.

He had the same tall, dark straightness as Gregori

26

and Stefan, and the same black eyes that even her half-brothers shared. He was good-looking, as Gregori was, and he was smiling a smile that showed perfect white teeth in the brown face. A smile that had a hint of mischief as well as appreciation of what he saw.

He moved quickly and met her at the foot of the stairs, one hand extended to take one of hers and carry the fingers to his lips. 'I am Nikolas Medopolis,' he announced in a low-pitched voice that was obviously meant to impress her with its seductive qualities, and confirmed her supposition that he was the youngest brother. 'You are Catherine Granger, are you not?'

'I am,' she agreed, and felt suddenly less apprehensive. This was someone who would not be averse to holding her hand, and not only metaphorically. Also, she felt sure, he would not be overawed by his impressive older brother. She smiled at him in relief. 'I'm very glad to meet you, Mr. Medopolis.'

Dark-fringed black eyes swept appreciatively over her features and lingered on her mouth, while his hand still held hers. 'You will become very confused if you call all of us Mr. Medopolis,' he told her softly. 'Therefore you must call me Nikolas, or Niki, you may choose which you prefer.' He offered her the choice with a solemnity that his gaze belied, and Catherine felt suddenly much lighter hearted.

'Thank you, Mr. – Nikolas.'

He kissed her fingers again lightly. 'I wish I could have been the one to come and fly you to our island,' he told her, seemingly in no hurry to join the rest of his family. 'But Stefan has – how do you say? – grounded me!'

'Oh, I see!'

Catherine was not at all sure that she should be standing out here in the hall, talking to Nikolas Medopolis like she was, not when Stefan had declared himself impatient to have her join him and his family for dinner, but she liked Nikolas instinctively. He was gallant and charming and he looked as if he would be fun, also she was in no hurry to be re-acquainted with his older brother.

'I am a menace to those on the ground as well as to those in the air,' Nikolas told her solemnly, and was again betrayed by the bright glitter in his eyes. 'That is what Stefan tells me, and he has forbidden me to take the aircraft up until I can learn more—' Expressive hands sought for words to express his brother's opinion. 'More control,' he decided at last, and Catherine smiled.

She could imagine the gist of the lecture and she sympathized, but at the same time wondered if she had been mistaken in thinking that he was any less amenable to his brother's wishes than Gregori was. Stefan Medopolis, she thought, would not only hold the whip hand but would not fail to use the whip when it was needed either.

'Do you always do as you're told?' she asked impulsively, and wondered how she could have asked such a personal and searching question of a complete stranger.

Not that Nikolas Medopolis seemed to mind in the

least, for he merely pulled a wry face and shrugged broad shoulders under an impeccably tailored white dinner jacket. 'It pays to do as Stefan says, as you will learn,' he told her, and Catherine frowned.

'I have no intention of learning any such thing,' she insisted, perhaps more sharply than she realized, for the suggestion came as something of a jolt to her. Why, she thought, did everyone behave as if she had come to this beautiful little island to stay?

'Oh!' Nikolas's eyes gleamed wickedly, and he took her hand again in his. 'You are a firework, eh?' He glanced at her bright hair and laughed softly. 'Perhaps you will make Stefan jump through hoops for a change, beautiful Katerina, but you will not find it easy! My brother is the head of his family, king of his island, and he will not easily be defied, not even by such a lovely rebel as you!'

It was the sound of a door opening somewhere behind them that brought them both round swiftly, almost guilty, and Catherine could have guessed who it was that came through the door. Stefan Medopolis stood for a moment in the doorway, a small frown drawing at his black brows when he saw them together, then he strode across to join them, and Catherine found her pulses fluttering nervously, as if she was afraid of him, which was quite ridiculous.

'We are waiting dinner,' he announced. 'You should have known that, Nikolas.'

'We were introducing ourselves,' Nikolas informed him with a definite hint of defiance, and his eyes glowed wickedly at Catherine.

'Then if you have done so perhaps you will join us,' Stefan told him. 'I wish to introduce Miss Granger to the rest of the family before we have dinner.'

'I'm sorry I kept you waiting.'

It annoyed Catherine to hear herself apologizing, and it annoyed her even more that she sounded so humble about it, but there was something about this man that inspired, if not servility, at least obedience. It was catching Nikolas's wicked black gaze that reminded her of her vow not to become as amenable to Stefan's wishes as the rest of them were.

'Come!'

The one word command seemed to give her little option but to follow him back across the hall to the room he had just left, with Nikolas walking close behind her. It was only when Stefan opened the door to admit them that she realized that the other three women in the room were wearing long, formal dresses and expensive jewellery.

The room itself gave her a momentary shock too, as the hall had done on first sight. It was long and high-ceilinged and seemed to be filled with light from the numerous hanging lamps suspended from the ceiling. They were worked in dull gold filigree in intricate shapes and added to the overall oriental impression that she had noticed too in her bedroom.

Among the rich furnishings and the formally dressed company she felt oddly out of place in her simple yellow dress, rather like a canary in a room full of peacocks. It was the women who gave her their full attention as she followed Stefan into the room, and she wished with all her heart that she had been able to dress more formally.

Stefan himself looked more impressive than ever in a dark dinner jacket with a white shirt that was unexpectedly, to Catherine at least, edged with a narrow white frilled border down the front of the broad chest it covered. The black trousers fitted to perfection and showed the strong, muscular length of his legs as he stood with his feet slightly apart while he introduced her to his mother.

Madame Medopolis, Catherine remembered from Maria, was Turkish and she was certainly much darker than any of her sons, except Stefan. It was from his mother, she realized at last, that he got those hawk-like, almost oriental features.

There was something in the old lady, however, that reminded Catherine of Maria, and the sharp black eyes under a fringe of grey hair had a kindly look, although they were speculative too. She had a serenity that Catherine recognized gratefully, amid the more tense and passionate manner of her family.

She inclined her head in greeting and accepted Catherine's hand, holding it for a moment while she studied her. 'You have brought my grandsons to me, Miss Granger,' she said in a thin, strongly accented voice that fell softly on Catherine's ear. 'I am very grateful to you for that.'

Catherine bit her lip, facing for the first time the fact that she had lost Paul and Alex to this dark, autocratic family. She looked down at her own hands, wondering if she had the self-control necessary to talk about her parting from the boys without resorting to tears.

'I – I hope they'll be as happy here as – as they have – as they have with me, Madame Medopolis,' she said. Her voice was low and husky and it was obvious that her self-control was slipping, and the old lady's hands reached out suddenly and clasped hers gently.

'There is no need to feel so unhappy about your change of home, my dear child,' she said softly. 'You will all be as happy here, I am quite sure.'

The silence that followed her words was almost tangible, and Catherine looked up at Stefan Medopolis in time to see him gently shaking his head at his mother, looking more regretful than angry. Then she looked back at the old lady and found her eyes downcast.

'Madame,' she began, 'I don't think you—'

'Come!'

A firm hand under her elbow would have steered her away from Madame Medopolis, but Catherine resisted it for a moment, looking up at her captor with a frown. 'I don't understand what—'

Again he interrupted her, that urgent hand relentless this time. 'I have told you there are things to discuss,' he said coolly. 'Now will you meet the rest of my family and leave discussions until the appropriate time?'

There was little else she could do in the face of such insistence, short of making a scene, and that was the last thing she wanted to do in this company. She found herself facing a tall and gauntly beautiful woman, a brunette with fine dark eyes that looked a little wary despite the smile she wore.

32

'Helen, this is Miss Catherine Granger,' Stefan announced precisely. 'Helen is my brother Gregori's wife, Miss Granger. She knew your father.'

It could have been Catherine's imagination, but it seemed to her that there was a hint of meaning behind those simple last words, and she could not miss the way Helen Medopolis's excellent teeth bit into her lower lip briefly.

'I thought you *all* knew my father,' Catherine said, feeling sorry for the woman, though for no good reason that she could think of. After all, she was beautiful and wealthy *and* married to the charming and gallant Gregori – there was little there to command pity, unless it was for having Stefan Medopolis for a brother-in-law.

'We did,' Stefan agreed briefly, and steered her away from his sister-in-law as firmly as he steered her away from his mother.

That inexorable hand under her elbow was beginning to vex her, and Catherine would have liked nothing better than to shrug it off and put its owner firmly in his place, but with a man like Stefan Medopolis such a thing was easier to consider than to do.

She smiled recognition of Gregori and passed on to the woman who stood beside him, a half empty glass of *ouzo* in one hand and a bright glittering look in her dark eyes as she looked at Stefan. She looked brittle and tense and rather unhappy.

'Elena,' Stefan introduced her in a cool, formal voice, 'this is Miss Catherine Granger; Miss Granger, my cousin, Elena Andreas.'

A chord of memory struck in Catherine's brain when she heard the name. Maria had never been very forthcoming about her family, but Catherine remembered her once mentioning that a cousin of their father's had hopes of seeing his daughter Elena betrothed to Stefan.

She was, in fact a second cousin, and it seemed her father's hopes had not yet materialized, for there was no sign of a ring on Elena Andrea's finger. It was evident too, that she had drunk far more than was wise, a fact that surprised Catherine, knowing the strictness of Greek families towards their womenfolk. Her gaze was all for Stefan, and the hand that briefly took Catherine's was trembling.

Catherine was given time only to make a brief conventional greeting, then that urging hand was again under her elbow, and urging her towards the door, following the rest of the family. Her escort retained his hold on her until they drew abreast of Nikolas, who smiled at her with a glint of laughter in his black eyes.

'Nikolas,' Stefan told him, 'you will take in Miss Granger, and you will please remember that she is a guest in our house.'

'Of course!'

Nikolas drooped one eyelid briefly at her behind Stefan's back and offered her his arm. 'Shall we go in?' he asked softly.

Had it not been for Nikolas, Catherine would have dreaded the meal, for she found the heady luxury of

34

her surroundings almost overpowering, and it was with relief that she finished her last course and rounded off the meal with some delicious fresh figs.

It all seemed so unreal somehow. The hanging lamps, like those in the salon, Turkish in origin, she guessed. The richness of heavy silver, gleaming voluptuously in the yellow light, and the heady perfume of flowers floating in huge bronze bowls in the centre of the table, like incense on the warm, still air. She felt as if she was part of the Arabian Nights instead of in a modern Greek home.

A long brown hand slid over hers as she swallowed the last of her figs and she looked up to see Nikolas's face quite close to her own, smiling, a small secret smile that hinted mischief.

'Will you walk in the gardens with me?' he whispered close to her ear, and instinctively Catherine glanced across at his eldest brother, remembering his earlier warning that she was a guest in their house. It was very obvious that Nikolas had none of his brother's formal reticence, and his invitation was made with no attempt to conceal his meaning. 'It is very beautiful out in the moonlight,' he urged.

'I'm sure it is,' Catherine smiled, nothing loath to make the most of his flattery. 'But I'm not sure I should just go for a walk when Mr Medopolis said he has something to discuss with me after dinner.'

'Oh, never mind Stefan!' Nikolas shrugged his elegant shoulders with a fine disregard for his formidable brother. 'He will know where to find you if he wants you.'

The rest of the party were drifting away from the table now, talking together in their own tongue now that they could see that Catherine was being entertained by Nikolas, and she smiled up at her good-looking tempter. 'Perhaps it will be all right for me to come for a little while,' she told him, and his smile betrayed that her answer was only the one he had expected. He would be used to having his own way, especially with the opposite sex, unless she was very much mistaken.

'It is *very* beautiful,' he assured her softly, and his hand slid under her arm, his fingers squeezing her soft skin gently, his face brushing close to hers as he leaned his dark head down to speak to her.

The night was like no other that Catherine had seen before. Deep and purple with a huge yellow moon sitting above a dark amethyst sea, a tracery of dark trees like black lace against the luminous sky. The scent of jasmine and hibiscus and a dozen other blossoms hung heavy on the still, soft air and the total effect was breathtaking. It could be dangerous too, she realized, in the company of a man like Nikolas Medopolis.

They walked through the trees where the darkness was more complete, but dappled with little patches of light where the brightness of the moon penetrated even the interlacing branches. The sea seemed to be all around them as it made a soft, sighing sound, rolling up on to the sandy beaches that came right to the edge of the trees.

It was so lovely that Catherine felt suddenly as if she could have cried, although of course it must have been not only the effect of the beauty around her, but also sheer tiredness that made her feel tearful. It had been a long, exciting day and she viewed it in retrospect with rather mixed feelings.

The opportunity to be in a place like this with a man as charming and attractive as Nikolas Medopolis was something to be grateful for, but at the same time, her reason for being there at all was to hand over Alex and Paul to their new guardian, and that was something she still found very hard to face.

'You are sad?'

Nikolas spoke softly in her ear and she shook her head hastily to deny it, although he must know how she felt about parting from the boys. 'How can anyone be sad in such surroundings?' she asked with a smile. 'I never dreamed it would be anything quite as lovely.'

She saw the glint of his white teeth as he smiled. 'You will like it here,' he promised, and Catherine frowned to hear that same expression of certainty again. As if he took it for granted that she would be staying on as well as the boys.

'I don't understand,' she said, 'why – why you and Madame Medopolis sound as if you think *I'm* staying on here as well.' She turned and looked up at him, sensing the sudden tension in the arm that supported hers. 'Why is it, Nikolas?'

'Nikolas!'

The voice was unmistakable and Catherine felt her heart give a sudden leap as if his arrival disturbed her, then she turned, with Nikolas, to face the newcomer. Nikolas pulling a wry face because he realized that his monopoly of her was at an end.

37

'You see,' he told her with a laugh. 'I told you he would know where to find you when he wanted you!'

'I wish to speak to Miss Granger alone,' Stefan told him, without apparently seeing the need to seek her opinion in the matter, and Nikolas squeezed her arm gently and smiled.

'I will see you again, Katerina!'

Catherine watched him make his way back to the house with regret, not only because she enjoyed his company but because she was a little apprehensive at being left alone with Stefan Medopolis. Not that she thought for one minute that he would make the kind of advances that Nikolas would have made, but because he made her feel small and strangely uneasy out there on the moonlit shore, and her own reactions disturbed her.

'Would you prefer to go back to the house and talk?' he asked quietly, and Catherine glanced up at him, startled for the moment at being consulted.

'No, no, it doesn't matter at all,' she said, in a slightly breathless voice.

For a moment he looked down at her with his dark eyes steady and glinting in the yellow light. 'Has my brother been stepping out of line already?' he asked then, in a cool quiet voice, and Catherine shook her head.

'No, of course not!'

A faint smile just touched his wide straight mouth for a brief moment, as if her vehemence amused him. 'You do not know Nikolas very well,' he told her, 'or you would not be so adamant in denying it.'

She turned away from him, her face shadowed by the overhanging trees, her red hair looking almost as black as his in the moonlight. 'I – I like Nikolas,' she said quietly. 'He's been very nice to me.'

'Of course,' he said coolly. 'You are a very lovely young woman. Now – if you do not mind, we will discuss matters that must be settled.'

Catherine turned and looked at him again, hoping she would not cry about losing the boys and make a complete fool of herself with this tall, chillingly practical man. 'There – there isn't really very much to discuss, is there, Mr. Medopolis?'

'I think so.' He turned her to face the sea again, but having achieved his object his hand was immediately withdrawn and did not linger caressingly, as Nikolas's had done.

The sea murmured softly, the creamy ruffled edges spreading gently over the white sand with barely a sound. There was a strangly haunting breathlessness about the place that she found oddly soothing but at the same time dangerously disturbing.

'Then – then I'd rather we stayed out here, if you don't mind,' she said. 'And if I feel – if I feel like—'

Her tiredness and the thought of losing the boys to this chilling stranger was almost too much for her suddenly, and she bit her lip, a mist of tears blurring her vision. 'If you feel like what, Miss Granger?' he asked, though not with the impatience she had expected.

Catherine brushed an impatient hand across her eyes and lifted her chin. She had vowed not to make a scene when the moment came, and she could have stuck to her vow, she felt sure, if only he had not insisted on discussing it in detail.

'Are you crying?' He asked the question softly, and for a second his dark head was bent while he looked into her eyes and saw the tell-tale glisten of tears, his breath warming her cheek as he spoke.

'I'm – I've made up my mind not to cry,' she declared, but was appalled to hear the way her voice was shaking. 'I shall just pack up and go and not – and not look back.'

'All of which is highly dramatic and quite unnecessary,' he informed her quietly, and Catherine looked up at him swiftly.

His features appeared even more stern and ruthless in the light of the big yellow moon, full of deep lines and with those black eyes as deep and unfathomable as the night itself. He was not a man it would be easy to explain her feelings to, and she felt quite sure he would only despise her for crying.

'You wouldn't understand,' she said in a small, tight voice. 'I – I love Alex and Paul, they're not only my brothers, I've brought them up for the past three and a half years. They're almost – almost like my own children.'

'Then why think of leaving them?'

Catherine blinked for a moment, wondering if she had dreamed the question or if she had misheard the words. He surely could not have meant what he just implied. 'I – I don't understand,' she said huskily.

'I would have thought that my family had given you

sufficient indication already,' he told her, with a hint of impatience. He moved away and leaned his tall figure against one of the slim cypress trees that stood dark against the night sky. 'I intend that you should stay here with them.'

'Until – until they settle in?'

She knew that was not what he meant at all, but she just could not believe anything else. Her heart was hammering at her ribs as if it would break from her body and she could not have said whether it was hope, excitement or apprehension that gave her that strangely sickening sensation in the pit of her stomach.

'I understand that you have no other relatives alive who are close to you,' he said in that cool matter-of-fact voice. 'You are far too young to be alone in the world, so you will stay here with your brothers.'

'But—' Catherine shook her head dazedly, her green eyes huge and shiny as she looked across at him. 'You can't mean to – to make yourself my guardian too,' she whispered. 'It doesn't make sense!'

'Of course it does not make sense,' he agreed shortly. 'But you will need a home, and since as you say you have been like a mother to your two brothers, the simplest solution is for you to stay with them here. You will be taken care of and they will be happier for having you here. I have arranged for the rest of your things to be brought over and you will find life as pleasant here as in London – possibly more so.'

Catherine stared at him, unable to grasp just how much of a change it would be for her to live here with the Medopolis family, or even why he thought she needed someone to look after her as if she was no older than the boys. She shook her head slowly.

'I'm not at all sure if – if I should,' she told him, and he frowned.

'I see no problem!'

She walked a little way along the shore, the soft, warm sand finding its way into her open shoes. There would be problems, not least of which would be Nikolas. Already he had warned his brother about behaving himself with her, and she felt sure he would not approve of any development in the relationship, which was bound to happen if she stayed on.

She turned again at last, and looked back at him, still with the cypress supporting his lean length. He looked poised, alert, and somehow exciting there in the moonlight like some dark statue, and he too offered another reason for not staying on. But then she put her two hands to her face and sighed.

'I'd love to stay on with the boys,' she admitted, and detected a brief gleam of white teeth in the dark face, as if he already saw her surrendering.

'Then there is nothing more to discuss!'

He left the support of the tree and stood upright, so much taller in the shifting shadows, his eyes glowing like coals in the moonlight, and she supposed he was waiting for her to join him, walk back to the house with him, but suddenly, as he stood there facing her, she experienced that faint flicker of recognition again.

'Where have I seen you before?' she asked, in a soft, puzzled voice, and he did not answer at once, but reached into his pocket and took out a cigarette and lit it.

'I did not expect you to remember,' he told her quietly. 'Last year you were with a party that was visiting an exhibition of Greek art in Birmingham, were you not?'

'Oh, of course!' It was all so clear suddenly, but the surprise was that he remembered her. 'I had a day out with a friend of mine and we went to the exhibition while her mother took care of the boys.'

'There were several pieces of mine there, on loan.' He drew on the cigarette and the red glow shone briefly, then died again. 'You missed your footing on the staircase and almost fell.'

Catherine nodded. She felt a strange curling sensation in her stomach suddenly when she remembered the strong hands that had broken her fall when she stumbled on the ornate marble staircase at the museum, and the dark, strong features of the man who had held her for a moment while she recovered her breath. Her friend, she recalled, had teased her about how slow she had been for not making the most of her chances.

She looked at him for a moment, a hundred different impressions going through her head. 'I – I had no idea who you were then,' she said.

'Nor I you,' he responded softly, and Catherine's heart gave a sudden, breathcatching leap, when she remembered the way he had hesitated, the look on his face when he first emerged from the room he was leaving and saw her in the hall.

'You – you recognized me – when I arrived?' she ventured, and he nodded.

'I have a very good memory for faces,' he said quietly. 'And your red hair is something of a distinction.'

'Not so much in England,' she denied with a smile. 'You find plenty of redheads about there.'

'Perhaps.' He moved across and put his hand under her arm, his fingertips lingeringly soft on her skin as he turned her in the direction of the house and walked beside her through the dark trees. 'But it is not only your red hair that distinguishes you, Miss Granger.'

Catherine did not question his meaning, but somehow that light, fingertip touch on her arm was much more evocative than Nikolas's more purposeful caress had been, and she questioned again her wisdom in agreeing to stay on.

CHAPTER THREE

CATHERINE found the prospect of staying on in the Medopolis house rather exciting, despite a certain apprehension. It was obviously going to be a complete change from anything she had known before, and she was almost as wide-eyed and eager as the boys were when she helped Casia to bath and dress them the following morning. The boys chattered incessantly and laughed with pleasure and excitement at the novelty of their new surroundings, so that the whole proceedings took on a holiday air that was infectious.

Catherine thought Casia found her own assistance with the boys rather an embarrassment, but she refused to be deterred from her usual tasks. For a while at least, the boys needed her presence to make them feel at home, and she had no intention of deserting them.

'You'll be meeting your grandmother this morning,' she told them while she brushed Paul's mop of black hair, and he turned his huge dark eyes on her, briefly worried by something strange, a small frown between his brows.

'Is she nice?' he asked bluntly, and Catherine gave the Greek woman a hasty glance to see if she had understood the question.

So far Casia had given no indication that she spoke any English, indeed she had said very little at all except a few words in her own tongue, but she smiled often and was plainly delighted with her charges. Also, after their initial suspicion, the boys seemed to have taken to her, which was a pretty good sign and something of a relief too.

'She's very nice,' Catherine assured Paul. 'I met her last night, and she's a very nice lady indeed. You'll like her.'

'Nicer than Grandmother Simmons?'

Catherine could not restrain a moue of regret. Her own maternal grandmother had been the only one the boys had ever known, and she had been so disapproving of her son-in-law's remarriage that she had made no secret of her dislike of his sons too.

'Much nicer than Grandmother Simmons,' Catherine promised with a smile.

'And will she like us?' Alex asked, as Casia vigorously brushed his thick dark hair.

This time it was Casia who answered, in a soft but strongly accented voice that reminded Catherine of the woman they were discussing. 'Your grandmama will love you very much,' she promised him with a smile. 'Many, many years Madame has waited to have a grandson.'

Catherine smiled, glad at last to have some closer contact with the woman. 'And now she will have two grandsons at once,' she said lightly. 'You'll both be very polite, won't you? You won't let me down when you meet all these new people?'

Two little black heads nodded in unison, although they looked a little undecided about meeting several new people at once, particularly Alex. It was something quite new to them to have so many strangers to face at one time, and Catherine prayed it would not all prove too overwhelming for them. Stefan Medopolis, she felt sure, would not approve of them hiding their heads in her skirts again.

'Right!' She sounded far more cheerful than she felt as she gave them each a last long look and took their hands in hers. 'Shall we go down to breakfast?'

Again they nodded in unison, and Casia watched them to the door, murmuring something softly in her own tongue, her head nodding approval. If she could have Casia on her side, Catherine thought, it would make matters so much easier for her, for she felt certain the woman was in good standing with her employer, and could do a lot to ease the boys into their new way of life.

The thought of perhaps not being allowed to see the boys very often had been one thing that had kept her awake for so long last night. Also, of course, she had lain there in the moonlit, oriental splendour of her bedroom and wondered if she could possibly have dreamed that incredible suggestion of Stefan Medopolis's. Or perhaps suggestion was not the right word, for he had spoken of the matter as if it was all cut and dried, and had even informed her that her belongings were on their way from England. Something she had been too stunned to protest about at the time.

There was a great deal she would have to consider, when she had had more time to get her bearings and to more fully understand what it would mean to live under the roof and the protection of Stefan Medopolis. In the meantime she meant to treat her stay as a holiday and no more, no matter what else Stefan Medopolis had in mind.

Breakfast was ready on a big, tiled patio, the table itself shaded by a bower of purple bougainvillea, and four members of the household were already seated round it. There was no sign of their host, however, and Catherine heaved an inward sigh of relief, as if she had been granted a respite.

Her appearance with the children coincided with the arrival of a young manservant bearing a tray with more hot rolls and butter and a fresh pot of coffee whose delicious fragrance reminded Catherine of how hungry she was.

Gregori and Nikolas Medopolis both rose politely to their feet when she approached, and Nikolas hastened to set a chair for her next to his own. His dark eyes issued an unmistakable invitation and they gleamed in approval of the pale yellow dress she wore.

'*Kalimera,* Katerina!' he murmured softly against her ear. 'You look very cool and beautiful this morning.'

He seemed not to notice Alex and Paul, for he neither spoke nor looked at them, and Catherine realized with a start that Nikolas Medopolis would acknowledge only those who interested him personally. Two small boys were of no consequence to him at all, therefore he ignored them.

Gregori approved of her appearance, it was evident, although his admiration was more restrained than his brother's, but his eyes too paid tribute to the flattery of the yellow dress with her creamy skin and copper-red hair. Helen, his wife, Catherine noticed, merely nodded silently, but her eyes revealed a kind of speculative curiosity that was hastily concealed by lowered lashes.

Ignoring Nikolas's invitation to sit beside him, Catherine took the boys round to where Madame Medopolis sat at the far end of the table. The old lady's eyes went immediately to her grandsons, but she spoke first to Catherine as good manners demanded.

'*Gun aydin,*' she said softly, her own native tongue coming most easily to her. 'I hope that you slept well, Miss Granger?'

'Very well, thank you, Madame Medopolis,' Catherine smiled. 'My room's quite beautiful, and very comfortable.'

'*Iyidir!*' The old lady nodded her satisfaction. 'I am glad that you find it so.' She gave her attention again to the two boys, and Catherine urged them forward.

'This is Alexander, *madame*,' she said, pushing him towards his grandmother with a hand in the small of his back and giving him the grandeur of his full name, something he seldom heard. 'Alex, this is your grandmother, Madame Medopolis.'

Alex murmured the polite words he had been taught and put his hand into the one that reached out to him, but he resisted its attempt to draw him closer to the old lady, and Catherine hastily introduced Paul. Usually Paul was a little less shy of meeting new people, and he would probably be more forthcoming.

Madame Medopolis, still holding Alex by one hand, took Paul's and shook it formally before drawing him closer, to stand by her knee with her arm around him. It was an emotional moment for the old lady, Catherine realized, and the dark, expressive eyes were misted over as she held her two grandsons by her side for the first time, murmuring soft words to them in her own tongue.

After a moment Paul put a friendly arm round her and smiled, his head cocked curiously at the sound of the strange words she spoke, while Catherine heaved a great sigh of relief. If Paul was willing to accept his new family, Alex would soon follow suit – he always did.

Nikolas, anticipating her undivided attention for the

rest of the morning, was less than pleased when Catherine told him that she meant to explore the island with the two boys. He was not only obviously disappointed but distinctly sulky about it, and he decided to follow some other distraction rather than join them, much to Catherine's disappointment. She found Nikolas Medopolis very attractive and had hoped to further their excellent beginnings of last night.

Even the brief-skirted and sleeveless yellow dress seemed too warm in the hot sun as they walked along a path that wound away from behind the Medopolis villa, and Catherine began to wish that she had brought a hat of some sort. The boys, on the other hand, seemed quite happy to run about as energetically as ever and already seemed very much at home on the island. Obviously they were going to settle in much more easily than she had anticipated.

It was never possible to be very far from the sea on Dakolis, but there were long stretches where one gained the impression that it was miles away. That was particularly true when they unexpectedly came upon a lush clearing in the dense growth of vegetation.

Hibiscus, oleander and bougainvillea clustered, colourful and exotic, among palms and orange and lemon trees, the same trees and plants that lined the road from the air-strip. The effect of the mingled scents and colours was so heady that Catherine felt herself in some kind of exotic paradise with no sense of time and so far forgot herself as to suddenly pull herself up when she glanced at her watch, realizing for the first time how easy it would be to get lost, even on a small island.

Dakolis was much bigger than she had imagined, and she stopped to wonder yet again at the incredible wealth of the Medopolis family that they could own not only this beautiful island, but another as well.

She called the boys to her, deciding to return before she went so far that she could not find her way back, but they were reluctant to come and begged for more time to explore the bordering trees round the clearing. Tolerant of their wishes, as always, she did not insist, but sat herself down thankfully on the warm, soft ground to wait for them.

Having failed to bring sunglasses with her as well as a hat, she closed her eyes against the brightness of the sun and leaned back on her hands, shaking her copper-coloured hair back from her face until it brushed her shoulders. It was so quiet here, a tranquil quietness broken only by the soft and mysterious sounds from the surrounding vegetation.

It was an incredibly beautiful place, and for the first time Catherine really began to think what it would be like to stay there indefinitely. It would surely be no hardship at all to live in such surroundings, and the boys very obviously enjoyed it.

She opened her eyes suddenly, realizing with a start that the shrill delight of the boys' voices was no longer part of the sounds around her. Scrambling hastily to her feet, she stood for a moment looking about her, with her heart hammering suddenly and inexplicably hard at her ribs, for surely there were no dangers in this lush paradise.

'Alex! Paul!'

Her voice sounded flat and quiet in the open, further deadened by the thickness of the vegetation. If they had gone any distance they would never hear her calling. Then panic gripped her for a moment when she remembered how close the ocean was and how adventurous little boys can be when they are left to their own devices.

Her distraction had been brief, but quite long enough for them to have made their way through the trees to the road and from there to the unfailing attraction of the sea. She had last seen them vanishing into the trees on the opposite side of the clearing to where she had been sitting, and without hesitation she ran across the soft yielding ground swiftly, her eyes anxious and her heart banging relentlessly away at her ribs as she went.

Its anxious pounding was accelerated suddenly and alarmingly when she suddenly ran, almost full pelt, into something huge and unexpected coming out from the cool shelter of the trees. Instinctively she let out a cry and one hand went to cover her mouth as she stepped back, dangerously unsteady on her feet.

If Stefan Medopolis was impressive on his own two feet, mounted on a tall, black Arab stallion he was even more so, and Catherine gazed up at him with something akin to fear in her eyes while he held the mettlesome creature in check to avoid knocking her down completely.

In the full light of day those dark, almost primitive features looked even more stern and relentless and her heart beat more quickly and anxiously when she realized how he would most likely react to the idea of her having let the boys wander off alone.

'Catherine?' Either he had taken her agreement to stay on as reason enough for him to use her christian name, or else surprise had made him descend to the familiarity.

His tall, straight figure sat the handsome animal with the pride and arrogance of a conqueror and for a moment Catherine's fear for the boys was forgotten in some new and disturbing sensation of awareness that stirred her pulses into violent action and brought swift, warm colour to her cheeks.

Cream-coloured trousers, close-fitting above short brown boots, emphasized the muscular length of his legs, and a cream shirt clung so closely to the broad, tanned torso that every ripple of movement under the golden brown skin showed through its thinness. He was looking down at her with a slight frown between his black brows and Catherine hastily brought herself back to the realization that the boys were missing.

'I – I seem to have lost track of the boys,' she confessed, and the frown instantly deepened ominously.

'You have lost them?'

Catherine nodded her red head, reluctantly honest. 'I'm afraid so.'

'Then we must find them at once! How could you be so foolish as to let them stray from you?'

He swung one long leg over the saddle and slid smoothly to the ground, towering over her and looking even more grim as he looked down at her. Of course she should have kept an eye on them, being in a strange place, and she really had no excuse at all if anything happened to them, but she could not help resenting the attitude he adopted and the pout of her lips showed it.

'Do you not realize,' he asked shortly, noting the pout and frowning over it impatiently, 'that on this side of the island the coast is rocky and very unsafe, even for an experienced swimmer? Two small boys would stand no chance if they should go near the water.'

'I – I didn't realize we *were* so near the water,' Catherine confessed. 'We seemed to be miles inland, well away from the shore.'

'One is always close to the water on an island of this size,' Stefan informed her shortly, contemptuous of her lack of knowledge. 'Come, we will search along the south side first!'

'Suppose you go one way and I go the other?' Catherine suggested, having no desire at all for the company of someone who obviously regarded her as criminally foolhardy.

'There is no need!' The black eyes again condemned her lack of perception. 'I have just ridden along the road from the north and I saw nothing of them. Come – we are wasting time!'

'But they can't have gone very far,' Catherine objected. 'I only closed my eyes for a few moments, that's all.'

Stefan turned his head and looked at her as they made their way into the trees. 'So!' he said. 'You were sleeping in the sun instead of watching your brothers!' He tightened his wide, straight mouth grimly. 'It is obvious that you must not be allowed to bring them out with you again, since you cannot take better care of them than this!'

Catherine's green eyes sparkled angrily as she half ran to keep pace with him, her breathing shortened by the effort. 'You have no right to say that!' she objected indignantly. 'I've taken care of them for over three years and you can't stop me from taking them with me if I choose to!'

One black brow rose and he half turned his head to look at her down his arrogant nose, his mouth firm and tight. 'You will find that I can,' he reminded her quietly but firmly. 'I am their legal guardian and if I say you do not take them out with you, then you do *not*! Is that understood?'

'You're not *my* legal guardian!' Catherine retorted swiftly, stung into rashness, her green eyes shining angrily. 'And if I choose to defy you, there's nothing you can do about it!'

For a moment he stopped short, turning to look down at her with such a deep glow of anger in his black eyes that she felt a shiver slip along her spine like an icy finger and a strange trembling sensation in her limbs.

'There is a great deal I can do about you, Catherine,' he said with dangerous quietness, 'as you will learn if you try my patience too far. No one defies me and escapes the consequences, so take warning and things will go easier for you!'

'I don't have to stay on your wretched island!'

Her defiance sounded childish, even to her own ears,

and she tingled with embarrassment when she saw the ever so slight tilt at one corner of his mouth that betrayed his amusement at her efforts to outface him. 'You do not, of course, have to stay here,' he told her quietly, once more striding out among the trees. 'You may go back to England whenever you wish, but you would find it difficult to explain to your brothers why you were leaving so abruptly. It would not be easy, I think, to get them to see your reasons, when you do not even know them yourself!'

Catherine said nothing. There was much she would like to have said, but instead she lapsed into a silence that was at once both sulky and defiant, as she tried to match his long stride through the trees towards the road. This was neither the time nor the place to indulge in personalities.

The colour and scents of the numerous flowers and trees around them made quarrelling in such a place seem like sacrilege. It was all so beautiful, and it all belonged to the man who now strode out slightly ahead of her, his tall powerful body as unrestrained and primitive as the lush growth around them.

The road appeared in front of them with almost startling suddenness and beyond it the deep sparkling blue of the ocean. Not rolling up gently as it did nearer the house, breaking into creamy lace on the white sand, but shattering into a million diamond-bright drops as it was hurled against the grey rocks that formed the shore at this point.

Catherine's blood ran cold when she realized just how dangerous it was for young children alone, especially children who were unused to the terrain as Alex and Paul were. She was forced to recognize how right Stefan Medopolis had been to make so much of her carelessness in letting them out of her sight, although it did nothing to console her.

'I see them!'

His words were short and clipped, but Catherine heaved a great sigh of relief when she heard them, and she would have rushed forward, calling to them if a restraining hand had not been placed firmly on her arm. It stilled her cry and held her unmoving as she looked up at him inquiringly.

'Wait here!' he instructed tersely. 'I will fetch them!'

'But—'

'Wait!'

The peremptory order gave her little choice, it seemed, although she was very tempted to argue, or at least to follow him as he strode along the rocky beach towards them. Alex and Paul were climbing on some dangerous-looking rocks about fifty yards ahead, and so far they had seen no one.

Then they saw and recognized Stefan and she could tell from the way they became suddenly still as he approached that they realized he was angry and that his anger concerned them. They were not yet fully aware of how much authority Stefan Medopolis had over them, but they would not be long in finding out, Catherine guessed.

It was not possible, at the distance, to tell what was said to them, but Catherine saw the boys climb down from the top of the rock to where Stefan could lift them down to stand in front of him, towering over them like an avenging giant. He bent and said something to each of them in turn and she saw their heads nod in unison, evidently impressed, then they looked along the beach and saw her for the first time.

Paul was away in a moment, running towards her, his face alight with some piece of news he was anxious to impart, and Catherine smiled instinctively as she held out her arms to him. But he was allowed to go no more than a couple of yards then she heard Stefan's deep, authoritative voice check him sharply in words she could not quite catch.

Paul stopped instantly, half turning, surprised and alarmed by the firm command, and Catherine could imagine his puzzled frown and the expression of wonderment in his huge, dark eyes as he looked first at the man who had stopped him from running to her, and then at her. Never in his young life had Paul been spoken to in such sharp tones.

Watching them, Catherine bit her lip, realizing that she knew nothing of their new guardian's ideas of discipline for small boys. She felt a sudden lurch of panic when she considered the possibility of his being as stern and cruel as his looks suggested, and determined to defend them at all costs.

Disregarding his instruction to her to stay where she was, she hurried towards them as they came along the rocky beach, and even at that distance she could see the subdued expressions on the two little faces as they walked beside their implacable guardian. How could she even think of going back and leaving them to his mercy?

It was Paul who smiled first, and it was such a tentative and wary smile, his huge eyes appealing as they could be, that Catherine felt a sudden need to swallow very hard. 'We ran,' Paul said simply, and glanced up at the tall stern figure beside him. 'We're sorry.'

'We're sorry,' Alex echoed, as if repeating a lesson, and Catherine was forced to the conclusion that they had been instructed to apologize to her for running off. Everyone was to have a share of the blame, it seemed, and Stefan Medopolis had delivered them all three a lecture on their sins.

'Oh, darlings—' she began, and would have gathered them into her arms, her relief to see them safe plain on her face, but a pair of large, strong hands took possession of their much smaller ones and they were drawn out of her reach.

They walked across the road, silent and a little downcast, although Catherine began to realize that the boys were as much curious as unhappy. The firm hand of authority from a man was a completely new experience for them, and they were not altogether sure how they felt about it at the moment, but nor were they completely against it.

'There will be no more exploring of the island unless you are accompanied by someone who is capable of keeping constant watch on you,' Stefan decreed firmly as they made their way through the vegetation towards the clearing. 'Do you understand me?'

'Yes, Mr. Med – Mop—' Even Alex's attempts to pronounce his name failed, and Paul did not even try.

'I am your uncle,' Stefan told them, still holding them firmly in those inescapable hands, although it meant his bending to accommodate their lack of inches. 'You should call me Uncle Stefan – you can manage that, hmm?'

His tone and his manner surprised Catherine, and she sensed a certain rapport between him and the boys that seemed to exclude her and gave her a sudden feeling of loneliness. A feeling that she sought to hide by pulling a huge red hibiscus from its plant and twirling it between her fingers.

The magnificent Arab stallion impatiently pawing the ground, caused great excitement, and admiration of him only served to exclude Catherine further, she felt, although Paul did turn and invite her to share their pleasure. She smiled, not daring to touch the silky black coat, for the animal looked as if it would rear at the slightest provocation.

'Don't get too close,' she warned instinctively, and Stefan Medopolis turned swiftly to frown at her.

'There is nothing to fear from horses, properly controlled,' he told her with a hint of impatience.

'But they're not used to horses.' Catherine was quickly on the defensive, a fact he recognized with another frown.

'I was afraid it would be so,' he said. 'And so of course neither of them can ride?'

It was, Catherine felt, a criticism, however oblique, of

herself as their guardian and she resented it. Her green eyes sparkled like jewels and she pushed back the red hair from her forehead and glared at him. 'They're neither of them very old yet,' she told him shortly.

'They are both older than I was when I learned to ride,' he told her abruptly. 'I will see to it that they are taught, at once.' The deep black gaze slid over her body and face slowly, from head to toe, and he raised an inquiring brow. 'Do you ride?' he asked.

Catherine shook her head. Her heart was hammering with sudden and alarming force at her ribs and she felt quite lightheaded at the many and disturbing things that slow scrutiny aroused in her. 'No,' she said. 'I've never learned.'

'Good!' His approval surprised her and she gazed at him for a moment, uncertainly. 'I dislike women who ride,' he explained blandly. 'It is a most unfeminine pastime.'

He was really the most arrogant and self-opinionated man Catherine had ever met, although he no doubt saw his opinions as quite reasonable, and she found herself left a little breathless by such unabashed self-confidence.

'Can we really learn to ride, Uncle – Uncle Stefan?' Surprisingly it was Alex who asked the question, and Stefan looked down at him from his vastly superior height with a slight smile.

'Of course you will learn to ride,' he told him. 'It is different for boys.'

Catherine never knew what prompted her to say what she did next, but some imp of mischief prompted her to be contrary and she lifted her chin, looking at him through the thickness of her lashes as he looked down at the boys.

'I'd like to learn too,' she said, and saw the dark disapproval in his black eyes when he spun round to face her.

The dark, rugged features had a relentless look and he said nothing for a moment, only looked down at her in silence, but she could see that a small pulse throbbed at his right temple, just below where the black hair grew thick and glossy over his brow.

'Merely for the pleasure of defying me?' he suggested softly, and Catherine felt herself colouring furiously at the accuracy of his guess. 'I think not,' he went on before she could confirm or deny it. 'Certainly you will not learn while you are on this island.'

'Your kingdom!' The jibe was impulsive and instinctive and she knew he would resent it even as she said it, but to her surprise his wide mouth tipped briefly into a tight smile that also glittered in his eyes.

'My kingdom,' he agreed softly. 'That is how Nikolas describes it, so I conclude that you have already decided to see me through his eyes.'

Catherine shook her head hastily to deny it, although she supposed that sooner or later she was bound to be influenced by Nikolas Medopolis's opinion of his brother if she decided to stay on Dakolis. 'I form my own opinions,' she declared firmly, determined not to be outfaced and he laughed shortly.

'On such short acquaintance?' he jeered softly. 'Even though I have taken the step of having you join my household, I have not yet formed an opinion of you as a person – favourable or otherwise. You might do me the courtesy of doing the same, instead of forming rash judgments based on my youngest brother's rather biased opinion of me.'

'I'm not influenced by your brother's opinion!' Catherine denied, but he merely shrugged his broad shoulders and turned away from her.

'In my country women do not argue,' he said coolly as he led the black stallion to a safe distance and swung himself up into the saddle once more, with an ease and grace that gave her a strange curling sensation in her stomach. The black eyes looked down at her steadily as he sat up there so straight and tall, his powerful golden-brown body easily discernible through the thin, cream-coloured shirt. 'There are many things you must learn, Catherine,' he told her quietly. 'But you are young – there is time.'

He said not another word, either to her or to the boys, and the three of them watched him ride away across the clearing. Catherine's pulses were throbbing wildly out of control at the sight of that tall, straight back, the strong legs and firm brown hands that controlled the stallion skilfully, and she was not altogether sure that it was anger that caused her such disturbance. Both man and animal were equally strong and powerful in their own ways, both as confident of their strength and doubtless of the admiration they aroused – they were a stunning combination.

Nothing about living on Dakolis was going to be very straightforward, Catherine faced that fact, but she suddenly felt more ready to accept any challenge that

Stefan Medopolis or his island cared to offer. He was right, there were many things she had to learn, and one of them was not to be so readily disturbed by the sheer, basic masculinity of her host.

CHAPTER FOUR

IT was almost three weeks now since Catherine's arrival on the island, and she was beginning to get a little more used to seeing less of the boys than she was accustomed to. It was not that they were any less fond of her, they made that quite plain by regaling her with their day's happenings as they had always done, but there was so much that was new and exciting for them to see and do that they were hardly conscious of her being excluded from their outings.

It was, she supposed, as well to make the break in this way, but it hurt a little at times when they were so willing to go off with Casia and with their two girl cousins on beach picnics and exploratory walks. Like today, Casia had taken all four children on yet another visit to the nearby beach and Catherine found herself alone but for the rather uneasy company of Helen Medopolis.

There was no reason at all why Helen should dislike her, as far as Catherine knew, but ever since Stefan had introduced them on the night of Catherine's arrival she had sensed a certain feeling of resentment in the other woman's manner towards her. Something that she felt was nothing to do with jealousy for Gregori's obvious liking for her.

There was a brittle, unhappy air about Helen that seemed to have no explanation. It was perhaps true that Gregori treated her with a kind of off-hand affection, rather than like a man who is deeply in love with his wife, but they seemed to get along well enough together, and they surely had no financial worries.

In view of her uneasiness in the company of Helen, Catherine deliberately chose a subject that she felt could not cause controversy of any sort. She spoke of the island and of its contrast to her former environment, since it seemed a safe enough subject, but even there Helen seemed distant and unenthusiastic.

'I have never been to England,' she said in her deep, flat voice when Catherine compared the climates. 'I cannot make a comparison.'

'You've lived here all your life?' Catherine asked, pulling an envious face. 'Oh, how lucky you are!'

'Lucky? You think so?' Helen's wide mouth twisted bitterly and when she laughed it was a short, harsh sound that had little to do with humour. 'I would like to have travelled the world, to have seen other countries, but—' She shrugged and her mouth twisted bitterly again. 'You think this island is a paradise, Catherine, but you have not yet seen the hidden bars that enclose a paradise like this! Kademolis, the island that I come from, is much like this one, and just as much a prison!'

'I – I'm sorry.'

It was difficult to know just what to say in the face of

such bitterness and resentment, and Catherine could not help feeling pity for her obvious unhappiness. At the same time it occurred to her that, given as many advantages as Helen Medopolis undoubtedly had, she could surely have done something more with her life than make it the hell she so obviously found it.

Dark, bright eyes looked at Catherine with that same hint of dislike in their depths as she made her apology. 'Why should *you* be sorry?' she asked, her voice sharply suspicious. 'You are not your father!'

'My father?'

Catherine stared at her, a faint uneasy suspicion stirring in her. The mention of her father had been totally unexpected and threw her off balance for a moment, but then she recalled Stefan's words to her on the night of her arrival. 'She knew your father', he had said about Helen, and even then she had been aware of some vague undercurrent, some allusion that obviously meant something to Helen, but nothing to Catherine.

Obviously her first instincts had been right, but before she could gather her thoughts together to say anything more, to question Helen about her meaning, she saw Nikolas coming across the patio towards them, and at the sight of him waved a welcoming hand. The welcome did not escape Helen's notice either and she laughed shortly as she watched her brother-in-law approaching.

'It is useless for you to think of Niki in *that* way,' she said bluntly, noting Catherine's smile for him. 'His future is planned out in the same way that mine and

66

Gregori's were, and no one upsets Stefan Medopolis's plans! Gregori married me, and Niki will marry the Pedopolous girl when the time is right. As for Stefan—' She laughed harshly. 'Who knows what Stefan will decide for himself? Certainly there will be no restriction of choice, and even if he chooses to marry Elena Andreas she is a fool if she thinks *she* could hold him!'

Nikolas, Catherine thought, must have caught those last bitter words, and his brief frown at his sister-in-law seemed to confirm it, but he said nothing to her. A moment later he was smiling and bending his sleek black head over Catherine's hand.

'At last I have found you,' he told her, ignoring Helen completely, after that brief frown.

'I didn't know you were looking for me,' Catherine told him, and smiled, partly in relief, she had to admit. Although she was curious, she was half afraid of any revelations Helen might make, although she could not have said why.

Nikolas's eyes gleamed darkly in his good-looking face as he looked down at her. 'Alas,' he said regretfully, 'I am no more than my brother's messenger. I had hoped that you would drive down with me to the north end of the island for a swim, but—' His expressive shoulders shrugged regret at the inevitability of yielding to his brother. 'Stefan has said that he wishes to see you at once in his study.'

'And you have to do as he tells you?' She could not resist the jibe, although she saw his dark eyes gleam with resentment.

'It does not pay anyone to defy Stefan,' he told her, one hand taking hers and squeezing the fingers hard, as if in rebuke. 'You have yet to learn that, Katerina.'

She was immediately contrite and smiled at him, seeking forgiveness, something he gave willingly enough and again squeezed her fingers, this time more gently. 'I'm sorry, Nikolas,' she said softly, aware that Helen was watching the byplay with an expression just short of a sneer, and once more wondering what it was that made her so unapproachable.

'You are forgiven!' Nikolas kissed the fingers he held. 'Now will you go and see Stefan before he thinks I have forgotten to tell you?'

Catherine nodded; her heart was beating with added urgency suddenly as she looked at Nikolas with a hint of anxiety in her eyes. 'Have you any idea why he wants to see me?' she asked.

Nikolas shrugged, his mouth twisting wryly into a smile. 'He does not tell me such things,' he said. 'But you do not need to look as if you have been summoned before a judge, my lovely! Even Stefan does not hold the powers of life and death, so you may go to him in safety!'

'I'm just curious, that's all,' Catherine assured him hastily, and Nikolas smiled again as he took her arm and turned her towards the house. She gave Helen a brief smile over her shoulder and walked with Nikolas across the patio, his hand moving softly and caressingly on her soft skin as they went, making a strange curling sensation in her stomach at the sensuousness of his touch. Nikolas could play havoc with her common sense when he put his mind to it.

'I have no doubt it is to talk about something quite dull, like business,' Nikolas said, and his dark eyes gleamed down at her warmly. 'Only Stefan would fail to see the wasted opportunity in such a thing.' He raised her hand and pressed the palm firmly to his mouth for a long moment while they still walked across the sunny patio to the house. 'I will be waiting when you leave him,' he promised softly.

'Nikolas—'

He kissed her fingers briefly and raised a curious brow, but on second thoughts Catherine shook her head, and went in search of Stefan Medopolis's study. This was no time to ask about Helen's connection with her father. Later, if the opportunity arose, she would ask Nikolas what it was that made Helen so bitter, and why she should suggest that it had something to do with Catherine's father.

The study was situated at the back of the house, and overlooked the same path that Catherine and the boys had taken on their initial exploration of the island, when the boys had gone missing. The view of palms, orange and lemon trees and the mass of other luxuriant vegetation was breathtaking seen through the high arched windows, and Catherine wondered how anyone could work in there with so many distractions.

The room itself was completely masculine, and curiously without nationality. It could have been a man's room almost anywhere in the world, with its deep, dark leather armchairs and the wide, businesslike desk with a swivel chair. The walls were white and the carpet underfoot a dark red with an intricate design in gold, and she recognized that it was probably Turkish, as so much of the decor of the house was. The sun's glare and heat was filtered by green shutters, but otherwise the room could have been in any English businessman's home or office.

When she went in Stefan Medopolis stood by one of the windows with his back to the room and his hands clasped behind him – a tall, shadowy figure in the filtered sunlight. His feet were planted firmly apart and in the light grey trousers he wore the muscles of his long legs showed taut and strong as if he braced himself for swift movement, while across the broad back a fine white shirt fell into loose folds with the backward pull of his arms.

Catherine stood for a moment in the doorway, feeling suddenly small and rather vulnerable in the white dress that clung to the soft fullness of her figure above the waist and flared out gently below it. Her heelless sandals were a definite disadvantage too, and she wished she had been prepared for this interview so that she could have appeared more formal and less like a schoolgirl called to the master's study.

Stefan swung round to face her suddenly and a faint smile crossed the dark, hawk-like features for a moment, as if in encouragement. 'Sit down, Catherine.' He indicated one of the armchairs, immediately across the desk from his own, and after a moment came and sat in the big swivel chair facing her.

For several seconds he said nothing, but the black eyes regarded her steadily and she found their scrutiny so disturbing that she uneasily broke the silence between them, without really knowing what she was saying. 'Nikolas said you wanted to see me,' she ventured. 'I – I can't think why – unless—'

'Unless?' The dark brows prompted her, but she shook her head.

'Why did you want to see me, Mr. Medopolis?'

He sought to hold her gaze, but Catherine was feeling more uneasy than she had ever felt in his presence before, and she thought perhaps Nikolas's words about his wasting opportunities had something to do with it. 'What do you think is my reason?' he asked, seemingly determined to make her answer him, and she held her hands together tightly in her lap, wishing they were not trembling so.

'I – I wonder if you're going to suggest that I leave the island and go back to England,' she said, and knew even before the words were out of her mouth that that was not it at all.

'I have made it quite plain to you that I wish you to stay here as part of my household,' he told her quietly. 'Why do you imagine that I would have such a sudden change of mind?'

'I—' Catherine shrugged and spread her hands helplessly. 'I don't really know,' she confessed, and was surprised to find herself relieved that it was not to dismiss her that he had sent for her. 'Except that I can't think of any other reason for you wanting to see me so urgently.'

She thought he smiled, but did not venture to look up and confirm it. 'It is to discuss your father's holdings in the Medopolis Line, in fact,' he told her quietly.

'Your shipping company?'

Catherine looked at him curiously for a moment, wondering why he should see fit to consult her on the matter. Her father had bought his way into the Medopolis family shipping business about the time of his marriage to Maria, and it was logical that the shares he had owned would now pass to Alex and Paul, so why he had thought it necessary to consult her when he was now the boys' guardian was beyond her.

A faint smile touched the wide mouth for a moment and he shook his head. 'The Medopolis Line is a family concern,' he corrected her quietly. 'It is not mine alone, Catherine.'

Catherine glanced at him from the thickness of her lashes, doubting that the family had a great deal to do with the running of the line, no matter if they were shareholders in the legal sense. Stefan would be the one to make all the decisions, she felt sure.

'But you're the big white chief,' she suggested with a hint of malice, and his mouth tightened briefly, as if he disliked the tone of her voice.

'I am the majority shareholder,' he agreed quietly. 'And as such I have the final vote on any important decisions, but it is still a family concern.' The black eyes looked at her steadily for a moment, and he leaned back in the swivel chair, steepled fingers propping his chin. 'You think of me as some kind of despot, do you not, Catherine?' he asked softly at last.

Catherine had seldom felt more uneasy in her life, and to make matters worse her pulses were responding

in the most disturbing way to the distinct and unde-
niable aura of masculinity that seemed to emanate
from him. Those strong brown hands that supported
his chin, and the vee of deeply tanned skin at the neck
of the white shirt – there were far too many things
about Stefan Medopolis that disturbed her. Things that
made him even more dangerous, though in a much
more mature way, than his brother Nikolas was. A
despot, he had suggested she thought him, and perhaps
it was not so far from the truth, but he was also a very
attractive man and that, at the moment, concerned her
more.

'Aren't you?' she challenged, trying hard not to be
submerged by the strength of either his personality or
his physical presence.

For a moment he did not answer, and then his broad
shoulders shrugged lightly and a glint of amusement
showed briefly in his black eyes. 'The word comes from
the Greek *despotēs*, meaning master,' he told her. 'So
in a way I suppose I *am*, on Dakolis at least.'

'Your kingdom!' she reminded him, and he inclined
his head in agreement.

'Since you share Nikolas's view of it – yes,' he agreed
softly.

Somehow, in this quiet unruffled mood, he seemed
even more disturbing, and Catherine sought to restore
normality by returning to the original matter. 'I – I still
don't quite understand why you want to discuss my
father's shares in the firm with me,' she said. 'They
belong to the boys now, surely, and *you're* their guardian.'

Stefan lowered his hands and leaned forward in the chair. The move brought his face closer, with only the width of the desk between them. Close enough for her to see that there were a number of fine lines that radiated from the corners of his eyes, as well as a scattering of grey in the thick black hair just above his ears.

The black eyes held hers steadily for a moment. 'Your father left the shares to you, Catherine,' he said quietly. 'Not to your brothers.'

'To – to me?'

She stared at him unbelievingly for several seconds, but for the past few years her father's legal affairs had been in the hands of the Medopolis lawyer, so Stefan was likely to have more knowledge of them than she was herself. He was probably one of his executors, if such a thing existed in Greece. Her own ignorance in such matters, even in England, was complete.

'Did you not know that he meant to leave them to you?' Stefan asked, and Catherine shook her head slowly.

'I haven't – I hadn't seen my father for three and a half years before he died,' she said in a small husky voice, still only half believing it. 'We never had much communication with one another.'

Stefan nodded, knowing that what she said must have been true, for he and his family had seen much more of George Granger during the last few years of his life than his wife and family had. 'I realize that,' he said quietly, and somehow managed to convey sympathy without actually uttering the words.

The sympathy, unspoken or not, affected her

strangely and she felt herself swallow hastily before she spoke. 'I didn't – I don't even know how well off he was,' she told him, facing the fact for the first time. She really had no idea how comfortably off her father had left her and the boys, herself especially, since the boys were now Stefan's responsibility.

For a moment Stefan said nothing, but sat with his hands clasped, the steepled fingers still supporting that strong, determined chin. Then he looked across at her and studied her narrowly. 'He was not a wealthy man,' he said slowly, as if he sought the right words to say what he had to say. 'But—' Broad, expressive shoulders shrugged such things off as relatively unimportant. 'He was comfortable, of course, and there are the shares.'

'Does – does having them make me a shareholder in the Medopolis Line?' Catherine asked, only now beginning to realize just what that could mean.

Stefan nodded, but it was obvious from the frown between his brows that the situation did not altogether suit him. 'Your father was admitted to the board of the company as the husband of my sister Maria,' he told her, and a faint inflection in his voice warned Catherine what was coming. 'Maria herself, of course, did not hold shares.'

She looked up, his reasons for wanting to talk to her, quite clear at last, and feeling quite unreasonably elated at the idea of being able to hold the whip-hand over Stefan Medopolis. It was much too good an opportunity to be wasted, and she looked at him from the shadow of her long lashes, her green eyes gleaming like jewels, her mouth curved into a small but satisfied smile.

'Of course,' she echoed softly. 'Maria was a woman, and in your world, Mr. Medopolis, women do not hold shares in *any* business, do they?'

He held her triumphant gaze for a moment, then got to his feet in a swift, lithe movement that somehow seemed threatening enough to make Catherine draw a sharp intake of breath and sit more upright in her chair. He strode across and once more stood in the window, as he had been when she first came into the room, adopting the same stance, with his hands behind his back and his feet planted firmly apart. It was a taut, oddly exciting stance that presented his broad back to her like a challenge.

'You appear to take it all very lightly,' he said, without turning his head, and his voice was cold and hard, as if he contained his anger only with difficulty. 'I am attempting to solve the matter of your father's shares to the best advantage of all concerned, but it seems you see it merely as a way of gaining some ridiculous feminine victory.'

Catherine could still scarcely believe that she was in a position where she could manipulate a man like Stefan Medopolis to suit her own ends, and the realization gave her a momentary sensation of power. He obviously wanted those shares and he believed she was prepared to hold on to them, even though she had not yet said as much. She wondered, not without a certain amount of trepidation, what he would do if she *did* hold on to them.

'I don't quite see how you can accuse me of that,' she told him in a deceptively meek voice, 'when you haven't even told me what your own proposals are yet.'

He swung round and looked at her steadily for a long moment, then strode back across the room and stood immediately in front of her, a proximity that was bound to have an unnerving effect, as he probably knew quite well. She kept her eyes downcast for a moment, and tried to do something about the way her pulses were responding to his being so close, and the way her hands were curled into her palms.

'Are you really interested in hearing what my proposals are?' he asked quietly, and Catherine nodded.

'Yes, of course, Mr. Medopolis.'

'Are you so formal with my brothers?' he asked, suddenly and sharply straying from the subject in hand, so that Catherine glanced up in startled surprise. He was, she suddenly realized, objecting to her use of his formal title, and she blinked for a moment, wondering why such a small thing should concern him, especially at a moment like this.

'I'm never sure what I should call you,' she said at last.

'You know my name!'

Catherine nodded, eyes downcast again, some imp of mischief prompting her as it had done once before when she had expressed a desire to learn to ride. The temptation to tease him was irresistible. 'Nikolas and the others call you Stefan,' she said, her voice softly meek. 'The children all call you Uncle Stefan.' She raised her green eyes and held his for a moment, brightly defiant. 'I wasn't sure which category I came into in the circumstances.'

He murmured something soft but obviously virulent in his own tongue, and Catherine hastily looked down again at her hands, her heart pounding wildly in a sudden flutter of panic. But instead of reaching out to strike her, as she half expected they would, those strong hands merely clenched themselves into tight balled fists at his sides, while he fought to control what was undoubtedly a fierce and passionate temper.

'You may use which you prefer,' he said at last in a harsh cold voice that shivered along her spine. 'But since you are so childish in your behaviour, it is perhaps more suitable that you call me uncle, as your brothers do!'

Catherine, with no intention of doing any such thing, looked up swiftly to refuse the suggestion, but the glitter in those black eyes was so fierce that she said nothing, instead sitting with her hands in her lap, feeling rather small.

'I'm – I'm sorry.' She felt that someone should break the awful silence that hung over them and, since he seemed prepared to do nothing more than stand over her, as if he was still deciding what to do with her, Catherine made the first move.

The hands, just within her range of vision, looked a little less tense, she thought, and the long fingers were now uncurled, but they still looked as if they might hit out at any minute. There was less tension in the tall, lean body too, and she took heart from it, raising her eyes to his stern face. It looked only a little more relenting and the wide mouth was still firm and harsh below that arrogant Turkish nose, but she took a chance.

'I'm sorry, Mr. Medopolis.'

'Stefan!'

'Stefan.' She repeated the name obediently, and saw a faint suggestion of softening in the stern features.

One hand reached out suddenly and she resisted the instinct to flinch away from it. Gently the long fingers touched her neck, then took a handful of copper-red hair and held it for a moment in a grip that made her wince.

'It is this – this fiery hair of yours, I think, that makes you so uncontrollable,' he said softly, and the depth and timbre of his voice set her heart hammering so violently against her ribs that she feared he must hear it.

'I'm not used to *be*ing controlled,' she said in a small, soft voice that she scarcely recognized as her own. 'It isn't the best way to get the most from people, you know.'

'You would teach me the ways of life?' One thumb pressed for a moment against her lips, then slid away, the long fingers running along her jaw and the side of her neck until the hand fell to his side again. 'You will learn,' he said softly, as if to himself. He stood beside her for a moment longer, then walked back round to his seat behind the desk. 'Can we now discuss the matter of your shares?' he asked quietly.

'Yes, of course!'

Somehow the sudden return to business matters came as something of an anti-climax, and Catherine felt vaguely disappointed that it was necessary. The problem of what to do about her shares was why he had asked her to come and see him, however, and sooner or later it would have to be discussed.

Stefan leaned back in his chair and regarded her for a moment down the length of his nose, his black eyes narrowed and speculative. 'I wish to buy those shares from you,' he said at last, in a cool, matter-of-fact voice, and Catherine considered for a moment.

It was plain now, of course, why he had wanted her to stay on in the first place. It had nothing at all to do with his concern about her being alone in the world, it had been done simply because she had inherited some shares in his shipping line and he wanted them under his control.

He had probably expected her to be so grateful to him for taking her into his family circle that she would hand them over without a second's thought. What dismayed her as much as anything about the whole thing was how much the realization disappointed her, and it was probably in defiance of her own feelings that she decided to dig in her heels. She was not going to part with the shares that were rightly hers to anyone – not even Stefan Medopolis.

'I don't want to sell them,' she said quietly, and saw the swift, dark frown that drew his brows together.

'But why on earth not?' Stefan demanded in a cold, stern voice that made her wonder if she was trying him too far. 'You do not understand such things and you are not a member of the Medopolis family!'

'Neither was my father!'

He was on his feet again and standing beside her, lean and hard, bending over her suddenly as if his mere physical presence would intimidate her sufficiently to make her change her mind. 'Your father was related to us through his marriage to my sister,' he reminded her.

'And he was a man, of course!' Catherine retorted, feeling her resistance already weakening.

'Aah!' Some rapid and virulent-sounding Greek words expressed his opinion of her stubbornness, and he stood there in front of her, leaning even closer now so that the warmth and tension of his body actually transmitted itself to her, making her shiver. 'You are stubborn,' he told her, the words short and harsh. 'But you will be sorry if you persist in this stubbornness, Catherine, I promise you that!'

If it had been possible to get up without finding herself even more disturbingly close to him, Catherine would have done so, but as it was she stayed where she was, feeling small and rather helpless in the face of his anger as he towered over her.

'You – you have no right to threaten me,' she ventured without looking up, and one large hand slid beneath her chin suddenly and jerked up her head.

'I have the right to do exactly as I please here,' he told her softly. 'This is my kingdom, do you not remember?'

'Then let me leave here,' she said in a sudden flutter of panic, and he curled his lips wryly, his fingers tightening on her chin.

'And leave your little brothers to my tender mercies?' he asked softly. 'I do not think you will do that, Catherine, will you?'

It was deadlock, Catherine realized that, but she was still not prepared to yield. It would have been too humiliating to let him have his way after the fight she had put up, and she felt that in some strange way he would have been disappointed in her if she had.

'Of course I'd much rather stay with them,' she admitted, 'but if you asked me to stay on here with them simply to get me to part with those shares, then you made a big mistake, Stefan.'

The black eyes had a hard, glittery look, but there was a curiously vulnerable look about his wide mouth suddenly which she did not understand at all. 'You think that?' he asked quietly, and Catherine hastily looked away.

'I – I don't know,' she confessed.

'You do me an injustice.'

She raised he eyes again, an unconsciously soft look about her as she accepted the assurance thankfully. 'Then I'm sorry I misjudged you,' she apologized in the same quiet voice, although her heart was thudding so hard at her side that she could hear it plainly and despaired of his doing so too. 'But it doesn't make any difference, Stefan. I'm not going to sell you those shares.'

'I see.' He let go her chin at last, but not suddenly and sharply, as if he was still angry. Instead his fingers slid along her jaw and across her cheek in a gesture that was as much a caress as anything Nikolas did, and she saw a deep, fathomless glow in his eyes that she had never seen before. 'Well,' he said softly, 'we shall see, hmm?'

'Stefan—' His words and his quiet acceptance made her curiously uneasy, and she looked up at him with wide, anxious eyes. His sudden smile, revealing strong white teeth in the dark face, gave him quite a different expression, one she had never seen before and which set her pulses fluttering uncontrollably again.

Two large hands cupped her face gently, their palms warm against her cheeks as he lifted her face to him. 'Fate has a way of evolving such matters,' he said softly. 'And you will not be leaving here, I know.' Briefly, unbelievably, the black head was bent over her and his mouth brushed her lips, hard and cool, and dizzying in its contact, bringing her momentarily against the warm, hard excitement of his body. 'We shall see,' he said again softly.

CHAPTER FIVE

Nikolas was looking at her with a kind of wry curiosity and Catherine was almost sorry she had confided in him. For several days now she had considered the idea of telling Nikolas the reason Stefan had sent for her that afternoon he had summoned her to the study, and today she had finally got around to telling him.

Whether Gregori, or even Madame Medopolis,

knew about her refusal to part with her shares in the Medopolis family firm, she had no way of knowing, but neither of them had so far betrayed any sign of disapproval; they were as unfailingly charming and courteous as ever.

Stefan himself was polite enough, she supposed, as far as good manners demanded, but he made no attempt to be any more friendly and his manner for most of the time was distinctly cool towards her. Only with the boys did he come close to relaxing a little, and that was only to be expected, even with him.

Nikolas had been curious about her session with Stefan, but he asked no questions, even when he met her afterwards as he had promised. Stefan's rather chilling manner towards her must have puzzled him if he did not know the circumstances, but Nikolas did not look for unpleasantnesses, and he had said nothing about it.

It was difficult to go back on her decision, having dug in her heels so hard about the shares her father had left her, but she sometimes wished she had been less tempted by sheer contrariness and had simply let Stefan buy them from her as he had wanted.

'Did you not realize that Stefan would expect you to let him have them back?' Nikolas asked.

He was stretched out lazily in the sun, and he sounded as if he disliked the matter of business being raised at all. It was also obvious that he considered her expecting his brother to react in any other than the way he had was optimistic to say the least.

'I didn't even know I *had* the shares until Stefan told

me about them,' Catherine said, not at all pleased with his apparently casual acceptance of Stefan's suggestion. 'I can't think why he left them to *me*, and I certainly wasn't prepared for Stefan to ask for them back.' She looked at him reproachfully. 'If only someone had seen fit to warn me what he had in mind before I saw him!'

Nikolas laughed softly, reaching out to touch her bare arm with a caressing finger that ran slowly up and down her soft skin. 'If you mean me, my lovely,' he told her, 'I did not know why Stefan wanted to see you, I told you so at the time, and even if I had known—' He shrugged lightly and Catherine began to realize that his attitude was no more than she should have expected.

It would not occur to Nikolas that there was anything at all unreasonable about Stefan wanting the shares returned to the family. For all his gallantry and his confessed readiness to please her, basically Nikolas shared his brother's attitude towards her sex. No doubt he saw her keeping the shares as not only unreasonable but quite unethical, although he would be much less angry about it than his brother had been.

She should really have known better than to expect his support, but she had felt the need to confide in someone and, since she spent more time in his company than anyone else's, he had seemed the logical person.

'Did you not know that your father had shares in the Medopolis Line?' Nikolas asked, and Catherine nodded.

'Yes, of course I knew,' she said. 'But as the boys

were Maria's sons, naturally I expected *them* to inherit the shares. I was stunned when Stefan told me they were mine.'

Nikolas chuckled deeply, his black eyes wickedly appreciating the idea of his brother's discomfiture. 'No more stunned that Stefan was when Miklos Tegarlos told him, I have no doubt,' he said. 'As your brothers' guardian he would automatically have had control of the shares they had inherited.'

Catherine turned her head and looked at him for a moment thoughtfully. 'Is that why he was so angry when I wouldn't let him have them?' she asked. 'Is he so desperate to have more shares to control?'

'No, no, no!' Nikolas shook his head and laughed dryly. 'He already holds a majority interest, he does not need the others to help him. No, my lovely, what angered Stefan was finding that he would have to deal with you, my lovely little fireball!' He laughed again and stretched like some sleek and dangerous cat. 'Oh, but I would have given much to have seen his face when you refused him! Women do not refuse my big brother anything, they simply bow their heads and accept that he is right.'

'Well, not me!' Catherine stuck out her chin, a soft colour in her cheeks when she realized how shocked Stefan must have been to have her deny him. 'And this is really no laughing matter, Nikolas,' she added firmly. 'I'm serious!'

She looked down at the long bronzed body stretched out beside her on the sand, its golden length broken only by a pair of brief white bathing shorts. His eyes were closed at the moment and his dark head resting on his upraised hands, clasped behind his head.

It was an idyllic place for bathing, down here at the far end of the island away from the house. One could imagine that there was no one else for miles on the gently shelving beach of white sand, surrounded by the same lush growth of trees and vegetation that seemed to cover a large part of the island.

The blue sea and a breeze just light enough to make the sun bearable, it was really quite silly of her to bring up matters like shares, and her disagreement with Stefan when there was so much here to enjoy, and Nikolas to enjoy it with. He was certainly one of the most attractive men she had ever met, and she felt quite sure that before much longer she would begin to imagine herself in love with him, no matter how unwise her common sense told her that would be.

As if he followed her thoughts, Nikolas opened his eyes and smiled at her, reaching up with one hand to pull her down to him, his dark eyes teasing her for her solemn face. 'Do not be so serious, my lovely,' he told her softly. 'Why do you not smile for me, hmm?'

'Nikolas—'

She bit her lip, her expression uncertain. Ever since Helen had told her that Nikolas was expected to marry a girl called Pedopolous when the time was right, she always felt uneasy at times like this. While Nikolas might have no conscience about playing fast and loose with his future wife somewhere in the background, Catherine was constantly aware of it. She also remembered that the match had been arranged by Stefan, and Stefan would not like having his plans upset, especially by an outsider.

A hand silenced her protest by brushing lightly across her lips, while the other held her firmly, strong fingers under her hair at the back of her neck slowly pulling her down closer to him. His strength was irresistible and his dark eyes, lazily half-closed, appreciated the curves of her body in a dark-yellow bikini.

'You are much too beautiful to be serious,' he murmured, and his grip was so insistent that her mouth was now only inches from his and his breath warm on her lips.

'Nikolas, I *have* to be serious about this!'

'Not with me!'

She was beginning to weaken, she realized it only too well, Nikolas always had that effect on her, but she was again reminded of that girl somewhere in the background, and she put her hands, palms down, on his chest in an effort to resist the pull of his arms, feeling the smooth golden skin warm and sensual to her touch.

'Katerina!' he whispered in a deep husky voice. 'Forget about shares and about Stefan, my lovely, hmm?' He pulled her mouth down to him and pressed his lips lightly, teasingly on hers. 'To please me, hmm?'

'Nikolas—'

He whispered words in Greek and the sound of them sent a shivering trickle of anticipation flicking along her spine. Then he turned suddenly so that the weight of his body held her pinned firmly to the shifting warmth of the sand, his mouth as warm and persuasive as those soft-spoken words in his own tongue.

Perhaps she was less transported than her persuader imagined, but it was Catherine who first became aware of the shadow that fell across them suddenly, coming between their entwined bodies and the brassy heat of the sun. She knew who it was too, even before she opened her eyes and saw him, or recognized the cool hardness of his voice.

'You have visitors, Nikolas!'

Nikolas was probably more perturbed by his brother's sudden appearance than he appeared to be, but he had a natural bravado that stood him in good stead at times like this. He turned lazily on to his back and gazed up at Stefan through heavy-lidded eyes.

'I have?' he asked with elaborate casualness. 'Now who could that be?'

'Leon Pedopolous and Athene are here,' Stefan informed him shortly, and Nikolas pulled a wry face.

'Oh, I see!' He got to his feet, bending to assist Catherine and brushing the clinging sand from his body. 'In that case I suppose I am expected to put in an appearance?'

'Of course!' Stefan agreed shortly. 'And in the circumstances it is as well that I came to find you myself instead of sending Dimitri.'

Nikolas ignored the reference and turned to smile ruefully at Catherine. 'I am sorry to spoil our afternoon, my lovely,' he told her, 'but—' A resigned shrug condemned his visitors to the realms of necessary evils. 'Hurry and dress, Katerina, and we will go.'

'You will go alone,' Stefan informed him in that same cool, disapproving voice. 'Why else do you imagine I took the trouble to fetch you myself? They do not know that you are with Catherine, and I do not intend that they shall. You will get dressed and drive back alone to see the Pedopolouses. I will drive back in a few minutes with Catherine.'

'But—' Nikolas started to protest, but meeting the hard, unrelenting glitter in his brother's eyes he changed his mind about objecting to the arrangement and merely shrugged his shoulders resignedly.

Dressing involved no more than pulling on a closely fitting crew-shirt and a pair of white trousers, and Catherine did not move while he dressed, but stood beside Stefan, brushing sand from herself for something to do to stop her hands trembling. Her reaction to such tyrannical behaviour surprised her, but she felt rather less angry than curiously elated by his insistence on taking her back with him.

Nikolas pulled on his shoes, ran careless hands through his thick dark hair and turned to look at her again, a small wry smile tilting his mouth at one corner and a bright gleam of resentment in his eyes for his brother's dominance. 'I will see you soon, my lovely,' he told her.

'You will entertain your fiancée and her father,' Stefan said firmly, before Catherine could even smile in response. 'I will see to it that Catherine returns safely to the house.' The black eyes turned on her for a moment, going slowly down and up again over her slim shape in its brief yellow bathing suit. 'I will also see that she is not bored without the benefit of your company.'

Nikolas said nothing, he merely placed sunglasses carefully on his nose, turned on his heel and walked to his car, then drove off at a speed that seemed to Catherine to be dangerously fast on such a narrow, twisting road. It was evident, however, that no matter how angry and resentful he might be, he still did as Stefan told him to, and once again Catherine wondered at the complete despotism of Stefan Medopolis as far as his family was concerned.

It was perhaps to deny his power over herself that she looked up at him with bright defiant eyes after they had watched Nikolas out of sight round the first bend. Her red head tipped back and she looked up at the dark, stern features for a moment without speaking, then she bent and picked up her sandals and pulled them on.

'I can walk back on my own, thank you,' she told him. 'You needn't bother waiting for me.'

'You will do no such thing.' His voice was cool and quiet, but it was adamant too, and Catherine stuck out her chin.

'Unlike Nikolas,' she stated firmly and clearly, 'I am not afraid of you, Stefan, nor do I have to do as you tell me! I'll walk back to the house!'

There was power in those broad shoulders and the lean hardness of his body looked as if it would be crushing in its strength, so that for a moment she felt a flicker of panic as she met the glowing anger in his black eyes.

'You will drive back with me,' he told her firmly.

91

'Do you imagine I would not have sent one of the servants to find you and Nikolas if there had not been good reason?'

'I – I suppose not,' Catherine admitted reluctantly.

His lip curled at her doubt. 'I am not in the habit of running around all over the island to discover where Nikolas has chosen to take you,' he informed her harshly. 'In this instance I did not want a servant involved. When the Pedopolouses arrived unexpectedly, Gregori agreed to meet them while I came to find Nikolas. He has told them that Nikolas was swimming alone and that I was out somewhere driving with you.'

'Oh, I see.'

Catherine did indeed see it all too plainly now. He did not want his plans for Nikolas upset, so he had gone to great pains to prevent Athene Pedopolous from discovering that her fiancé was with another woman. So much for his gallant insistence on seeing her back to the house – it was merely to lend weight to his deception.

'I do not think you see at all,' Stefan argued coolly, seeing her expression. 'Athene Pedopolous is – a plain child, and certainly no match for you, but she is very fond of Nikolas. I would not have the child upset by seeing him arrive back with someone like you!'

'Like me?' She spoke sharply, suspecting a veiled insult, but his dark brows rose in surprise at the query.

'If you were – less than pretty,' he said quietly, 'would you like to see your fiancé arrive home with a beautiful redhead?'

The compliment, so coolly and calmly paid, nevertheless did strange things to her senses. Her heart was beating much faster than normal, and a pulse in her forehead was throbbing wildly as she stood there on the white sand beside him. Her lack of clothing seemed only to make her feel more vulnerable and she looked vaguely round for her dress.

'I'd – I'd better get dressed,' she said, sounding quite alarmingly breathless.

'There is no hurry – not for us,' Stefan told her, and her heart gave another lurch at the familiar 'us'.

She looked up at him again, her eyes curious, the colour warm in her cheeks when she met the deep glow in those black eyes. 'You mean to play it out to the very last detail, don't you?' she asked. 'I am supposed to be out driving with you, so I must arrive back at the house with you!'

'It seems reasonable, I would have thought!'

Catherine shook her head, her eyes still more curious than resentful. 'Don't you ever get tired of running other people's lives for them?' she asked.

Rather surprisingly, he did not immediately lose his temper as she half expected he might, but his mouth tightened slightly and one brow questioned her meaning. 'Is that what you think I do?' he asked, and Catherine stared at him for a moment in disbelief.

'You surely *know* you do!' she said.

'I have certain responsibilities,' he admitted coolly. 'I have to make decisions – decisions that ensure that the best is done for all my family.'

'Even to arranging who they should marry, whether they agree or not?' she retorted, and could have bitten her tongue a moment later when she saw the cold anger of his expression.

She had seen him angry once before, when she had refused to part with her Medopolis shares to him, but now she had actually criticized his dealings with his family she had really passed the limits of discretion, she realized that.

He did not speak or move for a long moment and Catherine would have liked nothing better than to flee, but she was not even dressed, and there was nowhere for her to go. The whole island belonged to him – it was his kingdom, as she had told him on more than one occasion, and at last she realized what Helen had meant by its having hidden bars.

His eyes blazed down at her, dark and glittering as jet, and his mouth was straight and tight, almost cruel-looking, as were the big hands that he held tightly curled at his sides. 'You may thank your gods that you are not one of my family,' he told her in a cold, hard voice. 'Such interference in things that do not concern you is unpardonable and I will not tolerate it! However—' the broad shoulders shrugged briefly, 'since you are not of our people and not familiar with our ways I must allow you some mistakes. I will do nothing this time!'

Catherine felt her limbs and her whole body trembling as she faced him, wondering if such a scene could possibly be really happening, or if she was dreaming it. But that tall, ominous figure facing her was real enough and angry enough, and she felt suddenly helpless, despite her determination not to be bullied.

'You can't—' she began.

'Get dressed!' He bent and picked up the green dress she had not yet retrieved and handed it to her.

After a moment's hesitation, she took it. There seemed little option but to do as he said, and she stepped into the dress and pulled it up to her waist, drawing the sleeveless bodice over her arms, her mouth full and disapproving of the way he was treating her. The dress fastened at the back with a zip which she made no attempt to close because she knew she could not reach it herself, and she certainly had no intention of asking him to do it for her.

She wore no make-up and at the moment she was uncaring if her hair was untidy or not, so she merely turned her back on him with as much dignity as she could muster and started up the sandy slope towards the road beyond the trees.

'Catherine!' The voice brought her to a standstill again, and she turned to face him, her expression cool and unfriendly. 'You surely do not mean to go back to the house like that?'

He indicated the gaping back of her dress and Catherine shrugged, deliberately casual. 'There's nothing I can do about it,' she told him. 'I can't reach it myself.'

'And what would you have done if Nikolas had been with you?' he asked, and Catherine felt the colour in her cheeks as she hastily looked away.

Without another word, he turned her round, and

she shivered involuntarily when she felt the sensation of warmth from her body on her bare back as he moved closer. Her heart was hammering wildly in her breast and she experienced again that strange curling sensation in her stomach as his long, strong fingers manipulated the zip, running along her spine between the dress and her skin.

His dexterity set her wondering if it could possibly be that practice had made perfect, something she had never even considered until now, and which she hastily dismissed from her mind. It was not at all unlikely that Stefan behaved as any other man in his position, and she had heard some quite incredible stories about the exploits of the men on the Greek islands. Thinking of him in that way was oddly disturbing and she preferred to think of him merely as the boys' guardian and her own host for the time being.

As he lifted her hair from her neck and slid the fastener to the top, his fingers against her soft flesh had a sensual gentleness that was not only surprising, in view of his anger, but also alarmingly evocative. So much so that she shivered and bit her lip hard.

'Thank you!' Even her voice betrayed in her, a sudden and incredible awareness of him, and for a moment he neither moved nor spoke so that she felt her whole body trembling with a kind of panicky sense of anticipation.

She still had her back to him and his hands lay on her shoulders, the palms warm and hard, even though the strong fingers curled over her soft flesh in a hold that was not quite strong enough to hurt. 'You will not

say that you have been with Nikolas?' he said softly, and it was as much statement as question.

His voice was as deep and persuasive as Nikolas's had ever been and her senses responded to it much more violently. Her whole body felt weak and yielding and she had an irresistible urge to close her eyes and lean back against him.

'I don't—' She was unsure what her argument was to be and those strong hands on her shoulders prevented any movement that he did not permit. His fingers made no pretence of gentleness now as they tightened their grip on her shoulders.

'Do not make me angry again, Catherine,' he warned softly. 'Please – do as I say!' When she did not reply, he turned her slowly to face him and without even realizing she was doing it, she leaned against him with her copper-red head tipped back and exposing the creamy, vulnerable softness of her throat. His eyes glittered at her blackly for a moment, then he bent his head and put his lips to her throat. 'Catherine!'

His voice was strangely hoarse and his fingers closed in a steely grip on her arms, pulling her closer until she felt the powerful muscles of his body strainingly tense, almost as if he fought to resist. His mouth was hard and fierce and the arms that now crushed her to him allowed no movement but the lifting of her arms as they slid round his neck, and she closed her eyes at last.

The head-spinning delirium of it was brought to an abrupt end when he released her suddenly and stood looking down at her with such a bright glitter in his eyes that she felt herself trembling violently. Strong hands reached up and unclasped her fingers from the back of his head, pushing them down to her sides, and still he said nothing.

'Stefan!'

It was half inquiry, but for a moment she thought he was simply going to walk off and leave her when he turned his back. Instead he walked only a couple of yards away, then turned again and looked at her steadily until she lowered her own gaze.

'I am sorry,' he said quietly, and Catherine blinked at the unexpectedness of it.

'Oh, please don't—' she began hastily. His apologizing gave her a sense of anti-climax, and it was the last thing she wanted him to say.

'But I have to apologize,' he insisted, still in a remarkably cool, quiet voice. 'It was wrong to take advantage of you like that.'

'You didn't!' Catherine denied swiftly and impulsively, and glanced up at the strong, proud face with a hint of defiance. He was treating her as if she was a young girl who had never been kissed before, and that was far from the truth. She might never have indulged in promiscuity, but her twenty-one years had not been entirely bereft of experience and she had certainly been kissed before, although never in quite such a violently disturbing way, she had to admit. 'Nikolas wouldn't apologize for kissing me,' she told him, looking up through her thick lashes and wondering why on earth she was being so rash.

His dark brows drew together and the glitter in his eyes was from quite a different passion this time. Once again he was angry, and that was not what she had intended at all. 'I have no doubt that you speak from experience,' he said harshly. 'But Nikolas is not me, and I do not play children's games, Catherine!'

'And you think I do?' Something irresistible drove her on, although she knew she was being childishly vengeful, and it was obvious from his expression that Stefan thought so too.

'I do not know what kind of games you play,' he said, unexpectedly gentle, and for a moment one hand reached out and touched her cheek lightly in a gesture that was somehow moving in its gentleness. 'I do not think I have the right to find out,' he added softly.

'But, Stefan, I—' Catherine tried again to tell him that she had not objected to being kissed, that he had no need to apologize, but he would not listen.

He laid a finger over her lips and shook his head. 'Leave it, Catherine,' he begged softly. 'You do not know what you could do to me. At this moment I want considerably more from you than a few playful kisses on the sand, but regardless of your opinion of me, I do not simply take what I want when I want it.' He curled his strong hand over hers and drew her along with him. 'Come, we will go back to the house!'

CHAPTER SIX

It was unusual, so Nikolas rather crossly informed her one day, for Athene Pedopolous and her father to visit the island quite so often as they had done recently, and Catherine wondered uneasily if it had anything to do with her own presence in the house.

Although Stefan was firmly in favour of the marriage, it would surely be viewed even more favourably by Leon Pedopolous. To have his daughter married into the incredibly wealthy Medopolis family was quite an achievement, and any threat to the fulfilment of such an arrangement would not be taken lightly.

It was possible, of course, that Stefan had suggested more frequent visits to ensure that his younger brother did not forget his duties to his fiancée, but whoever was responsible, the visits did not suit Nikolas at all. Since the afternoon when Stefan had disturbed them on the beach, Athene and her father had called twice more in a little over a week. Not, perhaps, too often for a young man in love to see his fiancée, but Nikolas made no claim to being that.

Catherine missed his company too, for he was the one she had spent most time with, and without him she felt somewhat at a loss, now that the boys were with Casia so much. There was little encouragement from Helen to be friendly, and Gregori spent as much time as Stefan did flying back and forth to the mainland, visiting their various offices.

She was on her way up to her room one afternoon when she caught sight of Madame Medopolis from the corner of her eye, and turned to smile. She had developed a definite liking for the old lady and always found her charming and kindly, but it was something of a surprise when she realized that she was being beckoned across the hall.

The huge hall echoed to her footsteps on the ornate tiles as she changed direction and joined the old lady. Even after nearly five weeks in the house she still felt rather overawed by that great hall that reminded her of a Greek temple.

'*Madame?*' Catherine looked at her inquiringly, and Madame Medopolis smiled.

'If you would be so kind as to give me a few moments of your time, Katerina.'

Madame Medopolis was the only person, apart from Nikolas, who gave her the Greek version of her name, and Catherine wondered if it was because she found it easier to pronounce, for her English was much less fluent than any of her sons'.

'Yes, of course, *madame*!' She was puzzled, but she followed Madame Medopolis into her own private sitting-room, somewhere that very few people were allowed, so Nikolas had informed her once. She felt rather nervous and her heart was beating more rapidly than usual, although she could not imagine why that should be.

The room was much smaller than any Catherine had yet seen in the house, and it was completely Turkish in decor. Carpeted and cushioned in the most exquisite and luxurious fabrics, and heavy with the scents of the many blossoms that filled it and also with the aroma of coffee, it was exotic and somehow claustrophobic in its atmosphere.

Intricately carved bronze lamps hung from the ceiling and very little of the bright sunshine outside filtered in through the shuttered windows. It was very hot and rather oppressive, but at the same time fascinating, and Catherine looked around her with curious eyes.

'You like my room?' Madame Medopolis asked softly, and smiled as if she knew the answer well enough. 'You will take some coffee with me, perhaps?'

Catherine hastily shook her head, trying not to show by an involuntary grimace that Turkish coffee was not to her taste. 'Oh no, thank you, *madame*, really!' she said hastily. 'But I find your room fascinating, and I feel rather privileged being invited to visit you here.'

'My sons would not consider it a privilege, child,' the old lady told her with a wicked gleam of laughter in her sharp black eyes. 'They were only brought to this room when they had to be scolded!'

There were several chairs in the room, but, following her hostess's example, Catherine sat on one of the huge, plump cushions and curled her legs under her. 'I hope I'm not to be scolded, *madame*,' she said with a smile. 'I can't think of any reason why I should be, at the moment!'

In the shadowed room Madame Medopolis's sharp, dark features took on an almost sinister aspect, although she still smiled, and Catherine felt a strange flick of fear in the pit of her stomach. It was rather like being abducted and taken to an eastern harem, she felt, although the illusion was plainly ridiculous.

'Perhaps you are not to be scolded,' Madame Medopolis said softly, in her strongly accented voice. 'Although you are perhaps being a little foolish, child, are you not?'

Catherine looked across at her uneasily, her hands clasped together in her lap. More than a month on the island had taught her to expect the unexpected, but she did not at the moment know why the old lady had called her in and she was uneasy. 'I – I don't understand you, *madame*,' she said.

Madame Medopolis held her gaze for several seconds, a steady penetrating gaze that reminded Catherine irresistibly of Stefan. 'I think that you do, Katerina,' the old lady told her softly.

Still wary and uncertain, it crossed Catherine's mind that perhaps his mother had noticed Nikolas paying so much attention to her, and considered she should have been more discouraging. With that in mind she sought to clear herself of any ulterior motives.

'If you – if you're referring to Nikolas, *madame*,' she began, 'I can—'

'I am not talking of Nikolas,' Madame Medopolis said quietly, shaking her head. 'I am speaking of Stefan.'

'Stefan?'

It was impossible that anyone but herself and Stefan could know about that brief incident on the beach more than a week ago, but just the same she felt the colour flood into her face at the memory of it, and Madame Medopolis's sharp eyes noted it and narrowed shrewdly.

'You do not know to what I refer?' she asked softly, and Catherine hastily looked down at her hands.

'No, *madame*,' she said quietly.

For a moment the hot oppressive room was silent, and Catherine wished with all her heart that she had made some excuse not to come in here. Madame Medopolis was obviously bent on discovering just what it was she found so embarrassing that she blushed like a schoolgirl at the very thought of it.

'You blush charmingly, Katerina,' she said gently. 'But I cannot imagine why you should do so at the mere mention of my son's name.'

'Oh, Madame Medopolis, you're making something of nothing!' Catherine protested. 'I'm – I'm not blushing, I simply find it rather warm in here, that's all!'

'Ah! I see!' Small, slender hands deftly rearranged some mimosa in a huge pottery bowl beside her. 'Of course it is Nikolas that you find so attractive, is it not?' she asked.

'I like Nikolas, certainly,' Catherine agreed cautiously. 'But he's engaged to Miss Pedopolous, of course.'

'Of course,' the old lady echoed. 'And Athene is a charming girl, although I am afraid that Nikolas has yet to be convinced of that.'

'Perhaps if he had—' Catherine bit her lip hastily. It

would not do to criticize the arrangement to Madame Medopolis, for almost surely she would agree with Stefan, and she had already seen the effect of her criticism on him.

'You do not approve of our customs?' Madame Medopolis suggested softly, and her bright, dark eyes gleamed when she saw that she had guessed rightly. 'But it is a most satisfactory system, Katerina.'

'Maybe, for those brought up to it,' Catherine allowed.

'I know myself that such arrangements can bring great happiness,' the old lady assured her softly.

'Perhaps.' A sudden and uneasy suspicion entered Catherine's head, disturbing in its prospect, and she looked at the old lady warily. 'I – I hope Stefan doesn't try and – arrange anything like that for me, just the same!'

Again there was a shrewd, speculative look in those sharp, black eyes. 'I do not think he will do that,' she assured her. 'Although he will possibly influence your choice.'

'Never!' Catherine declared firmly, then blinked uneasily when the old lady smiled. 'That – that wasn't what you wanted to speak to me about, was it, Madame Medopolis?' Her heart was fluttering in a sudden panic and she was prepared to flee the island by any means, fair or foul, if Stefan had already decided to find her a bridegroom.

'No, child, that is not why I asked you to come here.'

'Then why, *madame*?'

There was a sudden firmness in the old lady's manner that reminded her again of Stefan, and Catherine regarded her uneasily. Something about those dark, hawkish features gave her a feeling of helplessness – the same she always had when she was with Stefan.

'You have some shares – some Medopolis shares,' the old lady said slowly, and Catherine felt her colour rise again, this time in anger.

'Yes, I do,' she agreed shortly, and her green eyes had a bright, defiant look that Madame Medopolis recognized at once.

'And you will not sell them to Stefan?'

'I will not,' Catherine agreed stubbornly.

She had been thinking lately along the lines of approaching Stefan about the shares. Thinking that perhaps she would swallow her pride and tell him that, on consideration, she had decided to part with them after all. But now that he had enlisted the aid of his mother, and sought to influence her by more devious means, she resented it bitterly.

'Katerina!' Gentle hands reached out and enfolded hers. Small and dry, they were nevertheless firm in their clasp, and the wrinkled face with its strong Turkish features leaned forward, seeking to persuade her. Kindly but determined. 'They are of no use to you, you cannot take your place at the meeting table as your father did.'

'I don't see why not!' Catherine argued, and Madame Medopolis shook her head, a small, wry smile on her lips.

'You do not speak or understand Greek, child. How would you follow what was said?' The thin fingers squeezed hers persuasively. 'Come, *bebek*, will you not let Stefan take care of such things?'

'On my behalf?' Such an idea had not occurred to her before and Catherine saw it as a way out. A solution that would ensure that neither she nor Stefan lost face.

'If that is the only way you will agree!'

Catherine looked at her steadily for a moment, puzzled to know just how Stefan would react to such a compromise. 'Does — is Stefan agreeable to those terms?' she asked, and Madame Medopolis's seamed brown face creased into a thousand lines when she smiled, her bright black eyes gleaming.

'It is a step along the right way,' she said softly.

Once again Athene Pedopolous and her father were to join the family for dinner, and once more Catherine had the opportunity of observing the girl who was eventually to be Nikolas's wife if Stefan had his way.

As Stefan had said, she was a plain girl, although perhaps plain was rather too unkind a word, for she had a certain wistful charm that could prove very endearing. Fairly tall, she was inclined to plumpness, but she had the beautiful dark eyes of her race and they seldom left Nikolas's good-looking face whenever she was near him.

Such frankness made it obvious that, once again, Stefan had been right. Except that Athene was not merely fond of Nikolas, she adored him, and knowing him as she did, Catherine could only feel sorry for her. Stefan had said, that day on the beach, that he would not have her upset by seeing Nikolas arrive at the house with Catherine, but if Athene were to marry him she would almost certainly have to resign herself to her handsome husband having a roving eye!

As was usual when there were extra people for dinner, the seating was rearranged and Catherine no longer sat next to Nikolas but between Gregori and Mr. Pedopolous. Nikolas sat opposite to her and next to Athene, something he regarded with an unflattering air of long-suffering.

When there were visitors too, it was customary to wear more formal dress and Catherine always secretly admired Stefan when he appeared in evening dress. Being so tall and slim he carried off the dinner jacket and frilled shirt better than any man she had ever seen, even Nikolas. It gave him a somewhat romantic air, despite his arrogance, or perhaps because of it. With his stern, hawkish features he looked every inch the eastern despot, and without realizing it Catherine curled her hands into their palms at the sight of him.

Mr. Pedopolous had said very little to her in the few times they had met, but then he was usually engaged in earnest conversation with his host who sat next to him at the head of the table. Several times, however, Catherine had been aware that his sharp, black gaze had noted Nikolas's attempts to catch her eye. It was very unfair of Nikolas when she was doing her best to behave sensibly, and she kept her own gaze firmly averted.

The dining-room, always a grand room, seemed to take on an added grandeur when there were extra guests. The linen was dazzlingly white, and elaborate silver caught the light and gleamed richly, while huge ornate bowls of floating blossoms lent their heady scent to the exotic atmosphere of the big room. Even after several weeks, Catherine still found it all rather unreal.

The food was a mixture of Greek and Turkish and there was an unbelievable quantity of both. Delicacies like *feta*, a strange rather sour-tasting cheese, and vine leaves stuffed with a variety of meats and vegetables that went under the deceptively simple name of *dolmas. Moussaka* and *keftedes*, some highly spiced meatballs which were a particular favourite of Catherine's, were followed by exotic pastries and the most delicious Turkish delight.

The coffee was very strong and made in the Turkish way, and Catherine refused it when it was offered, for it was a taste she simply could not acquire. The whole incredible banquet was finished off with mounds of fresh fruit of every description.

Unlike the night of her arrival, when she had felt so embarrassingly out of place in a short simple dress, tonight Catherine wore a long full gown with wide sleeves. It was a deep jade green with gold embroidery, and it did wonderful things for her colouring.

Nikolas had presented it to her after one of his infrequent trips to Cyprus to visit one of the company's offices, and she was not at all sure that she should have accepted such a gift, but the temptation had been too much for her.

Tonight was the first time she had worn it, and in view of the identity of their guests, she was not at all sure that she was wise to do so. Nikolas had scarcely taken his eyes off her the entire evening and it was obvious that he read something meaningful into her wearing it.

She had not missed Stefan's brief, but unmistakable, appreciation of it either when she came down to join the rest of the party for drinks before dinner. A swift approving study by those black eyes had set her pulses racing in a way that both alarmed and excited her. Perhaps it was the effect of the dress, but she had to admit to being quite deliberately provocative the once or twice she had caught Stefan's gaze on her during dinner, and his half curious, half discouraging looks had given her a sense of elation that made her quite light-headed.

'Do you like our country, Miss Granger?'

Leon Pedopolous's question took her momentarily by surprise and Catherine turned rather a vague gaze on him for a second before she answered. 'I – I haven't seen anything of Greece itself yet, Mr. Pedopolous,' she told him with a smile. 'I landed in Nicosia when I arrived, but I was there only a few minutes, and since I came to Dakolis I haven't been off the island at all.'

She thought Stefan looked vaguely disapproving, as if he took her remark as a criticism of his hospitality. Helen, she noticed briefly, looked unmistakably I-told-you-so, but she had not meant to imply criticism, and she looked at Stefan again through the thickness of her lashes, wondering if she should try and convince him of that.

'I did not realize that you wished to leave the island,' he said, in his cool, quiet voice. 'If you would like to go across to Cyprus for a change, there is no reason why you cannot do so.'

Catherine smiled at him hopefully, her green eyes shining with enthusiasm for the idea. Her heart was again hammering heavily at her ribs when he met and held her gaze, and no amount of self-derision made any difference. Maybe she was a complete and utter fool, but the effect of those black eyes on her was infinitely disturbing, and it never for a moment occurred to her that she was a free agent and could have demanded to leave the island any time she wanted to.

'Oh, I'd love to go, Stefan, if it could be arranged,' she told him.

'I can—' Nikolas began, but a warning frown from his brother silenced him swiftly and efficiently.

'I have some papers for you to sign,' Stefan said. 'If you can be ready tomorrow morning when I leave for Cyprus you may come with me and so—' the broad shoulders shrugged as he sought the elusive adage, 'kill two birds with one stone?'

'Papers?' Catherine looked at him, puzzled, and Stefan raised a brow.

'You have made some concession concerning the shares, I believe,' he said quietly.

'Oh! Oh yes, of course!' She had completely forgotten about her rather unnerving interview with Madame Medopolis and its outcome, a couple of days before, but apparently Stefan meant to have the matter signed and sealed as soon as possible.

'You have not changed your mind?'

The black eyes challenged her to do so, and Catherine hastily shook her head, glancing at Madame Medopolis. There was a serene, untroubled look on the old lady's brown face, and somehow it worried Catherine, although she could not have said why.

Leon Pedopolous had been taking quite an interest in the exchange, and after a moment or two he turned to Catherine curiously, a small polite smile on his bearded face. 'You have shares in the Medopolis Line, Miss Granger?' he asked, and Catherine would have sworn that the question irritated Stefan, judging by the swift frown that drew his black brows together.

'I – I have some,' Catherine admitted. 'My father left them to me.'

'Ah yes, of course, your father!' He flicked a narrow-eyed glance at Stefan. 'It is most unusual for women – ladies to take an interest in such things, Miss Granger,' he said quietly, and Madame Medopolis laughed softly and reached out a hand to touch Catherine's gently.

'All sorts of things change in this world, Leon,' she said in her thin strongly accented voice. 'And Catherine is a sensible girl.'

'So it would seem,' Stefan endorsed his mother's opinion with a wry smile and once again the black eyes caught Catherine's gaze and sent a trickle of excitement along her spine that made her fingers curl into her palms. 'You will be ready in time in the morning, I hope, Catherine!'

'Oh, I'll be ready,' Catherine assured him quickly. 'What time are you leaving?'

'A little after ten o'clock.' The black gaze sought hers yet again. 'Wear something cool,' he told her. 'It can be very hot in town at this time of year.'

'Yes. Yes, of course!'

It was quite incredible, the excitement she felt at the idea of going across to Cyprus with Stefan, and it was no use telling herself that it was merely the thought of seeing somewhere different for a change. Her excitement stemmed purely and simply from the idea of spending several hours in Stefan's company and she made no attempt to deny it to herself.

Nikolas took it much less agreeably, however, and he did not disguise the fact that he disliked the idea of not being allowed to take her himself. When the Pedopolouses had left, later on that evening, he came out to find her in the gardens and looked so sulky and out of temper that she barely restrained a smile.

When he caught up with her as she walked among the cypress trees that skirted the ocean, his fingers curled possessively around her upper arm, and he leaned his dark head close to hers. His breath was warm against her ear when he spoke, and Catherine wished he would not indulge in such intimacy when it was only minutes since Athene left the island. It made her feel so terribly guilty when she thought of Athene and her adoration of him.

'Tell me that you would rather go with me, Katerina,' Nikolas begged, his dark eyes glistening earnestly in the moonlight.

'But I don't mind going with Stefan,' she told him, and laughed softly when she saw his moue of reproach. 'Anyway, it's as much a business trip as anything else, Nikolas, although I've no doubt I'll enjoy myself too.'

'With Stefan?' He pulled another face. 'You should be warned about my big brother, Katerina. He is not like me, not one bit.'

'He's more serious than you are, certainly,' Catherine allowed, not too sure that she followed his meaning correctly.

'He is also not for young girls like you,' Nikolas informed her solemnly, and his dark eyes glowed meaningly in the moonlight. It was obvious that he was trying to convey something to her and Catherine wished she did not have an uneasy inkling what it was.

'You're not making much sense to me,' she told him, emerging from the shadow of the trees and into the light of a huge yellow moon that rode low in a dark amethyst sky.

Nikolas's fingers curled more tightly round her upper arm and he leaned his face close to hers. 'Do you not think I have seen those looks you give to Stefan when you think that no one can see you, my lovely?' he asked softly, close to her ear, and Catherine felt the colour in her cheeks as she hastily moved away from him, pulling her arm from his grasp.

'You've a strong imagination, Nikolas,' she told him in a small, breathless voice. 'There's nothing special about – about the way I look at Stefan – why should you think there is?'

Nikolas shrugged his broad shoulders. 'Women find him attractive, I know,' he said. 'But not your sort of women, Katerina, you are not of his world.'

'But I am of yours? Is that what you're saying?' Catherine asked, an edge of uncertainty on her voice when she realized that what he said was true.

'Of course, my lovely!'

'Even when your fiancée is hurt every time you look at *me* the way you do?' she asked, and knew she was being unduly harsh, but it was the way she felt at the moment. 'You're not a bit fair to Athene, Nikolas, not a bit fair.'

Nikolas's good-looking face looked sulky again and he tightened his hold on her arm again as they walked along the edge of that creamy, lace-edged tide. 'She is Stefan's choice,' he said harshly. 'Let Stefan marry her!'

The rather cruel retort raised other doubts in Catherine's mind, and she barely looked at the breathtaking surroundings about them as she kicked white sand into little grooves with her sandalled feet. 'I thought Stefan was to marry Elena Andreas,' she said quietly. 'Maria said so and so has Helen, since I've been here.'

'But neither would dare have said a word about it within Stefan's hearing,' Nikolas told her shortly. 'Stefan arranges the lives of others, but he does not allow anyone to interfere in his own plans!'

Catherine could not have given any sane reason for it, but her heart was hammering away like a wild thing in her breast and she looked up suddenly at the big yellow moon in the sky and felt a strange sensation of elation. 'Does that mean he *isn't* going to marry Miss Andreas?' she asked, and Nikolas shrugged.

'Who knows what Stefan has in mind?' he asked gloomily. 'I sometimes wish he *would* marry and then perhaps he would have less time to make our lives miserable!'

Catherine thought again about Helen and her bitterness towards her brother-in-law. Evidently she had not wanted to marry Gregori, although if she had to make a choice Catherine would have said that the middle brother was by far the most kind and considerate of the three.

'Helen – Helen isn't always very happy, is she?' she asked, treading a little warily, for she was not at all sure how Nikolas would react to her mentioning Gregori and Helen as an example.

Nikolas's dark eyes were turned on her for a moment, but he said nothing, and she wondered if he had indeed taken offence at the suggestion. Then he put an arm round her shoulders and hugged her close for a second, his face close to hers as he spoke, so quietly she only just heard. 'You do not know about Helen, do you?' he asked.

Again Catherine recalled that first night she had arrived on the island. That rather meaningful mention of her father that Stefan had made when he introduced Helen, and Helen's reaction. 'I know – I *think* there's something about Helen that makes her rather – rather sad,' she ventured. 'I don't know what it is, but I suspect it has something to do – to do with my father.'

There! It was said now, and if he wanted to tell her, Nikolas could do so, or he could tell her she was mistaken and that would be an end to it. Nikolas, however, was more seriously thoughtful than she had ever seen him, and he walked in silence for a while. A silence that Catherine was curiously loath to break.

'I don't know how you know,' he said at last quietly. 'I don't think Helen would have told you, and I am quite sure that Stefan would not do so—'

'I guessed,' Catherine told him softly. 'I put two and two together, from various things I'd heard and noticed.'

'Oh, I see!' For a moment the familiar flash of white smile in the dark face complimented her astuteness. 'Well, you are quite right about it, my lovely. There *was* something between Helen and your father.'

'Something between them?' Catherine had not expected anything quite so blunt as Nikolas's statement, and she looked at him for a moment uncertainly.

Nikolas smiled a little wryly. 'You sound very shocked, Katerina,' he told her. 'But you did not know your father very well, I think, did you?'

'I hardly knew him at all,' Catherine admitted. 'I saw very little of him.'

'But you must know that he spent a lot of time in Greece?'

Catherine nodded. 'Yes, I knew that. He liked the country and he liked the people.'

'He met Gregori at the home of a mutual friend,' Nikolas explained, 'and he was invited across to the island for dinner one night. Helen was here, as Gregori's fiancée, and George, your father, seemed to take her eye immediately.' He smiled again, rather ruefully as he spoke of her father's shortcomings. 'I think he was flattered, for Helen *is* a good-looking girl and she was no more than twenty-two years old then.'

'About ten years younger than my father would have been at that time,' Catherine said soft-voiced, and he nodded.

'I think he found her admiration very flattering,' he said. 'And Helen took him much more seriously than he intended.'

'Poor Helen!' Catherine said softly, and Nikolas nodded.

'Poor Helen!' he echoed wryly. 'But she should have known that she could not win. She was betrothed to Gregori, and nothing would be allowed to upset that arrangement!'

'Stefan's plans!' Catherine said. 'No wonder she talks about them so bitterly.'

'Not only Stefan's plans,' Nikolas told her, unexpectedly loyal to his brother. 'Leon Pedopolous must have made the first move in the arrangement, it is always so, and neither Helen nor Gregori objected at first or Stefan would not have agreed.'

'But Maria!' She recalled her lovely, sad-eyed young stepmother. 'How did my father come to marry Maria?'

Nikolas shrugged, his dark eyes distant, as if he too had memories of his sister. 'She loved him,' he said simply. 'And I think George was quite fond of her in his own way.'

Catherine, for the first time in her life, felt a real bitterness in her heart for her father's behaviour. 'And of course he got the Medopolis Line shares as well, didn't he?' she asked, and Nikolas nodded.

'It is customary for girls to bring a house as part of their dowry,' he told her. 'But since Maria was not to live in her own country, the shares were given instead.'

'Oh, God!' Catherine closed her eyes, the lids prickling with tears for the fate of her exiled stepmother. 'It – it's not much better than slavery, is it?'

Nikolas looked at her curiously, his dark eyes studying her features, so small and pale in the light of that huge moon, her eyes glinting with unshed tears. 'I don't think Maria thought of it like that,' he said softly, and put a gentle hand on her cheek, drawing her face close to his, his arm still encircling her shoulders. 'You're much too solemn-faced about such things, my lovely. Maria married the man she loved, even if she did not see very much of him after the wedding. It was more than a lot of girls can do.'

'Nikolas!' She turned in the circle of his arm and looked up at him anxiously, her green eyes dark and shining in the moonlight. 'He – Stefan wouldn't – he wouldn't try and do anything like that to me, would he?'

'Marry you off, do you mean?' Nikolas looked as if he was considering the matter quite seriously for a moment, then he gathered her into his arms and his mouth was only inches from hers, his breath warm on her lips. 'If he ever does try such a thing, my lovely,' he said softly, 'we will run away together and defy him! I swear it!'

CHAPTER SEVEN

DESPITE her doubts about him and her condemnation of him the night before, Catherine still felt an unquenchable sense of excitement as she prepared to visit Nicosia with Stefan. The boys eyed her eagerly when she told them she was flying across to Cyprus, and immediately asked to go too, a request she would have granted without hesitation, had she been going with anyone but Stefan. As it was she sought to discourage them.

'It's only a business trip,' she promised, while they watched her with their big, anxious dark eyes. 'I have to sign some silly papers for your uncle, that's all, then I'll be coming back.'

'We like flying,' Alex ventured, encouraged by his brother's nodding head. 'Couldn't you ask Uncle Stefan if we can come too, Catine?'

Catherine hesitated, her loyalties divided for the first time in her life, and a little disturbed by it. She was really looking forward to the trip with Stefan, no matter how businesslike it was, and she found herself oddly unwilling to share his company, even with the boys. At the same time she felt rather guilty about leaving them behind while she went out and enjoyed herself.

'I'll speak to your uncle about it,' she promised, hastily subduing her conscience, for it was almost certain that he would refuse to take them.

She dressed carefully for the occasion, conscious that it was a part business trip, but remembering also that Stefan had told her to wear something cool. The dress she wore was plain, and uncluttered enough to satisfy the more formal part of the trip, and the spicy-brown colour of the linen flattered her colouring and gave her creamy-light skin a faintly golden glow. Light shoes, that were suitable for either town or country, matched her dress very well, and she gave her reflection a last satisfied glance before going to see the boys again.

Casia was with them and the woman gave her a rather odd look when she told her what she had in mind. 'Mr. Medopolis will not take them, I think,' she said in her soft, pedantic English, and Catherine sighed.

'I'm afraid you're probably right, Casia,' she told her. 'But there's no harm in trying.'

She took the boys, one by each hand, and went downstairs with them, their chatter echoing on the wide staircase as they came down into the hall, and just as they reached the foot of the stairs Stefan came out from one of the rooms. He stopped for a moment and looked at them, all three, his black eyes narrowed, then he strode across and stood looking down at Catherine steadily.

His own attire was much less businesslike than she had expected, and it struck her for the first time that he did not mean to spend all day in the office and leave her to her own devices, an aspect that brought a whole new set of possibilities to mind.

Cream trousers and jacket fitted his lean frame as impeccably as ever, and a brown shirt, opened at the neck, lent an air of informality. His dark, hawkish features gave little hope of it being a lighthearted outing, however, and she felt some of her enthusiastic anticipation evaporating already.

'What is it you expect me to do?' he asked without preliminaries, and throwing the onus firmly on to her.

Catherine held his gaze for only a moment before she looked away. 'I – I wondered if we could take Alex and Paul as well,' she ventured, and knew the suggestion was unacceptable even before she made it.

He looked down at the two little boys and shook his head. 'I am sorry,' he told them, and actually sounded as if he meant it. 'We cannot take you this time, little ones – perhaps another time, hmm?'

His gentleness with the boys always intrigued her, and she knew Alex and Paul were already very fond of him. Paul particularly, with his more extrovert nature, made no secret of the fact that he found his new uncle very much to his liking. He had fitted into his new environment very well and seemed very happy with it. But it was Paul, of course, who made most fuss about not being allowed to go with them.

He very often reminded Catherine of Nikolas, and she saw it now in the huge reproachful eyes that he turned up to his uncle, and the slightly sulky bottom lip. 'Come too,' he demanded. 'Me and Alex want to come too!'

'You cannot come too,' Stefan told him quietly but firmly. 'I have said you may not.'

Paul eyed him hopefully for a moment longer, then evidently recognized him for the relentless opponent he was and gave his attention to Catherine as a more amenable subject. 'Catine,' he said in his most soulful voice, 'can't we come too?'

Catherine had never felt so guilty in her life as she did at this moment, and she would have considered pleading their case, no matter what her own feelings were, had it been anyone but Stefan. With that implacable black gaze fixed on her and waiting to see her response, she could do no more than crouch down beside Paul's stocky little figure and put a consoling arm round him.

'I'm sorry, darling,' she told him, 'but it just isn't possible – not this time.'

Paul's lip thrust out even farther and a suspicious brightness filled his eyes. 'Why can't we come?' he asked, his voice shaking pathetically.

'Because—' She looked up at Stefan helplessly, and saw a hint of impatience in his eyes.

'Because I have said you may not!' he told Paul shortly, then shook his head hastily, as if he regretted having been so abrupt. When Catherine stood up again, he brought his own towering inches down nearer their level and put a large hand on each small boy. 'While I am gone I shall be doing something about getting you some ponies of your own,' he promised, in a much gentler voice, his dark face relaxed into a smile.

'You will like that, hmm?'

'*Real* ponies?' Paul's eyes were wide and round, while Alex watched the proceedings with growing wonder.

'Of course, real ponies!'

'Me *and* Alex?' Paul looked briefly at his silent brother. Despite his year and a half seniority Alex was always quite happy to let Paul be the spokesman.

'You *and* Alexander,' Stefan agreed, giving Alex his full name as he always did.

Paul looked up at Catherine again, almost resigned to staying behind now that he thought he knew the reason for the trip. 'Is Catine goin' to choose?' he asked, and Stefan laughed softly as he shook his head.

He straightened up, lifting Paul in his great hands and holding him at eye-level while white teeth gleamed in his dark face. 'But no! Choosing horses is man's work, little one,' he said. 'We do not leave such things to women!'

Catherine felt the colour in her cheeks as she bit her tongue hard to stop herself from objecting to that bit of sheer male arrogance, but Paul was quite happy to go along with it.

'Horses!' he crowed delightedly as he was set on his feet once more. 'We're going to get horses, Alex!'

Alex, Catherine thought, was less noisy in his enthusiasm. He had never had Paul's lively and insatiable interest in everything new, and he was much more gentle. Paul, she realized with a start, was as much like Stefan as he was like Nikolas, while Alex had his mother's more gentle nature. His silence did not go unnoticed by his uncle either, for Stefan looked down at him with a small frown drawing at his black brows.

'Are you not excited about having your own pony, Alexander?' he asked, and Alex glanced first at Catherine before nodding his head.

'Yes, Uncle Stefan.'

Stefan said nothing for a moment, then he shook his head, that hint of impatience showing itself again. 'But you do not have your brother's courage, hmm?' he suggested shortly, and Catherine felt bound to protest.

'Oh, Stefan, no!' She looked down at Alex's solemn little face and would have crouched beside him, offered consolation for that harsh judgment, but Alex himself was meeting that dark implacable gaze with a steadiness that startled her.

'I'll ride my horse too,' he said, in a firm little voice. 'I will, Uncle Stefan!'

A large hand reached out and touched his head for a moment and Stefan murmured quiet words in his own tongue, smiling down at the boy. Catherine had only time to wonder at the sense of understanding between the two of them before the black eyes gave their attention again to her, sweeping over her swiftly and searchingly.

'If you are quite ready, Catherine,' he said, 'we will leave.'

There were a number of things that Catherine wanted to say to Stefan as they flew over that incredibly blue sea, but she was so entranced with everything she saw that she said nothing about his being so harsh with Alex, or about his scathing remark about her sex when he spoke to Paul. Instead she looked down at the ruffled coastline and the sun-soaked landscape of Cyprus and exclaimed her delight in what she saw.

'I will make a Greek islander of you yet,' Stefan told her with a tight little smile, as he banked the plane to land at Nicosia.

His efficiency at handling the plane she took as just one more proof of his apparent infallibility. He seemed to excel at everything he did and somehow it gave her rather an inferiority complex. He was well known at the airport, as was inevitable, and she felt a certain unexpected sense of pride when she noted the appreciative stares of some women travellers watching his lithe, easy stride and the proud, hawklike features made darker by the light suit he wore. A man like Stefan Medopolis would be irresistible to women, and he would take it all in his stride, perhaps even treat their admiration with a kind of cool disdain.

Landing at Nicosia gave her a strange sense of freedom too, although it was true she had merely exchanged one island for another and her jailer, if he could be called that, was still with her. Cyprus was much bigger than Dakolis and it was not ruled by Stefan Medopolis, that was in its favour.

There were almond and apple trees laden with ripening fruit, and fragrance in the air that defied identification. Trees and a variety of musky and spicy scents seemed to be the first and deepest impression of

Nicosia that Catherine got.

They drove along streets that were both narrow and wide, sunny and shadowed. Where tall white buildings made canyons of busy streets, wrought iron balconies overhung the bustling scene below, and shuttered windows set wide open to catch the very most of what breeze there was. There were even people sitting on straight-backed chairs on the pavements, reading newspapers or simply gossiping in the sun.

It was all new, different and exciting and Catherine tried to miss nothing as they drove to where Stefan had his office. Her complete enthralment with everything she saw seemed to satisfy her companion, and the one time she ventured to look directly at him she received such a smile in response that it took minutes for her pulses to settle down to normal again.

The office itself proved rather less sumptuous than she would have expected, but it was comfortable enough and blessedly cool after the heat outside. An electric fan did its share towards that, but also the windows here were wide open above the street as in the other buildings she had seen, the slatted shutters pushed right back.

The furniture was old and dark and rather beautiful, similar to that at the house on Dakolis, and Stefan seated himself behind a large desk that could have been the twin to the one in his study on the island. A clerk in the outer office had eyed her with discreet but unmistakable approval as they came through, and Catherine's smile had brought a responding gleam of white teeth in the brown, good-looking face.

'We will get the business of signing completed first,' Stefan decided as soon as they were both seated, and he pushed a bell on his desk to summon the same young clerk Catherine had noticed.

A few rapid instructions in Greek and the man disappeared to return a few seconds later with a bundle of papers which he laid carefully in front of his employer. Evidently everything was in readiness for their visit, and Catherine was not really surprised by it. Stefan would never do anything on the spur of the moment, she felt sure, particularly a business transaction. At least, she thought wryly, her shares would be in good hands, for Stefan would be a conscientious trustee of her property.

The clerk had remained, on Stefan's instructions, and now Stefan got up from the swivel chair behind the desk and indicated that Catherine should take his place. The papers in front of her were completely incomprehensible to her, for they were in Greek, and Stefan did not miss her swift upward look of curiosity.

'I know you do not understand Greek,' he told her with a hint of his usual impatience. 'But there has been no time yet to have them drawn up in English too. I will have a translation of the documents done as soon as possible and you may have them.'

'Thank you.' She was seemingly meek in her thanks, but she was glad he had correctly interpreted her look. It would not do to let him think she was a complete innocent when it came to business matters.

He murmured a few words to the clerk and once

more he disappeared and returned with the young typist from the outer office. With only a brief hesitation she signed her name in the place where Stefan's long forefinger indicated. Stefan himself signed, and then the clerk and the young typist. It was all signed and legal, and in a way she felt a certain sense of relief.

Stefan thanked his staff politely in their own tongue, and dismissed them, then he turned and looked at Catherine as he folded the papers into a neat oblong. 'I am glad you have been sensible, Catherine,' he said quietly, and she shrugged.

'I don't mind you doing the business part of it for me,' she told him. 'As Madame Medopolis pointed out, I don't speak Greek and I wouldn't have been able to attend meetings and things like that. This way we both get our own way!'

For several seconds he said nothing and she watched him while he carried the bundle of papers across to a rather antiquated wall safe and put them away. It was when he turned to face her again that Catherine began to have a feeling of doubt. He sat himself on the edge of the desk beside her, one suede-clad foot swinging easily, one arm across his thigh, his hands clasped together between his knees, leaning towards her.

'Catherine,' he said quietly, 'do you know what it is that you have just signed?'

Catherine looked up at him suspiciously, her red head shaking slowly back and forth as if she sought to deny what she was already sure she knew. 'Tell me,' she said in a husky voice.

'You have signed your shares over to me!'

She stared at him for a moment, her green eyes suddenly bright with anger, as much for her own gullibility as for his deception. 'You cheated me!' she accused. 'You know I don't speak Greek and you deliberately had those papers drawn up in a language I didn't understand so that I wouldn't know what you were doing! You – ohh!' She got to her feet, her hands clenched hard to restrain an impulse she had to hit out at him.

'I did *not* cheat you!' His voice sounded so cool and quiet in contrast to her own that it simply served to add fuel to her own anger. 'I have only now realized that you did not *know* you were signing them over to me.'

'I thought I was giving you leave to deal with them on my behalf,' Catherine told him in a tight angry voice. 'And I refuse to believe you weren't fully aware of what you were doing!'

'You think that I deliberately set out to cheat you?'

He had a taut and chillingly dangerous look about him, and Catherine felt a sudden flutter of panic in her breast. He was close enough to reach out and strike her for her accusations if he had a mind to, and she found herself watching those strong, dark hands with a kind of fascinated fear.

'I – I don't see how you can have *not* known what I expected,' she said in a small husky voice. 'I told Madame Medopolis what my idea was, and she agreed that you would be satisfied with acting as my representative.'

'Your representative!' The black eyes scorned such a submissive role, as she should have known he would.

'In my own company? My mother knows me better that to imagine I would even dream of accepting such a position, Catherine! You misunderstood her, I think!'

'I didn't misunderstand at all!' Catherine faced him angrily, her cheeks brightly pink and the glint of fury in her eyes that made them appear even more green than usual. 'Madame Medopolis said that if that was the only way I would agree, it was all right. She said that it—'

'I do not wish to hear a verbatim report of everything you and my mother said to one another,' he interrupted her impatiently. 'You obviously misunderstood one another, and so you have done something you had no real wish to do.'

'I want that paper—'

'You want!' The interruption was more violent this time and his lips curled on her demand. 'It is done now, and you might as well accept it with good grace, Catherine!'

'You have no right! You cheated me!'

'I have every right!' he declared coldly, 'and I did *not* cheat you!' A hand fastened like a steel band round her right wrist and the black eyes were only inches away, blazingly angry. 'You will not make such accusations again, do you hear me?'

'Let me go!'

She snatched at her wrist, but the steely fingers did not relinquish their hold and she succeeded only in hurting her own arm. 'Be quiet!' His voice was stern and cold, but subdued, and a moment later she realized why. 'Do you think I want my staff to know that you are behaving like a spoiled child because you have lost something you had no real right to in the first place?'

'Are you sure it isn't because you don't want them to know that you cheated me out of something my father left me in his will?' she retaliated. 'You knew what you were doing, Stefan, and I refuse to believe you didn't!'

'And I was certain you knew what *you* were doing!' It was impossible for such violent passion to last, and after a moment or two she felt the grip on her wrist ease fractionally, and the eyes that studied her were less blazingly angry and more steady. A look much more disconcerting to meet. 'I did not cheat you, Catherine,' he told her quietly, and in a tone she felt bound to believe, despite her conviction.

'I – I can't believe it.' The denial had much less conviction now and he recognized it.

'I thought you had agreed to let me have the shares, and I had the papers drawn up accordingly. I suppose,' he added with surprising humility, 'that I should have consulted you again myself, but I was afraid you would change your mind yet again if I did.'

The touch of his hand on her wrist was having the inevitable effect on her senses now that it was less cruel, and she felt her pulses thudding uneasily when his thumb began to gently caress the soft skin of her inner arm. That alarming sense of awareness made her tremble like a leaf as she looked at him for a moment before saying anything.

'Did – did you really think I'd changed my mind

about letting you have those shares?' she asked at last. It was easy enough, when she thought back, to recall Madame Medopolis's quiet acceptance of her decision and wonder at it. A step in the right direction, she had called it, and Catherine realized what an excellent excuse her supposed lack of English could prove to be on occasion.

'Of course I believed you had changed your mind,' he said quietly. 'I would not have let you sign that paper otherwise. You do me an injustice, Catherine.'

'I'm – I'm sorry.' She looked down at the spot where his shirt opened at the neck to show the muscular brown throat with its throbbing pulse, and felt her fingers curl into her palms. That caressing thumb on her wrist was having the most devastating effect on her self-control and she felt sure her trembling must be evident to him.

Briefly the white teeth showed in a smile and he raised one brow in question. 'Shall we have lunch?' he suggested quietly. 'And forget our differences.'

'Stefan—' She wanted to suggest that a new set of papers could be drawn up, but before she could put it into words, he leaned over and kissed her gently on her mouth, his lips firm and persuasive and making her forget what she wanted to say.

The restaurant he took her to was quite small, but it had a curiously intimate air that Catherine found intriguing, and Stefan's company brought her many curious glances. It was obvious he was known, although few spoke to him, the recognition being all on the other side. No doubt the Medopolis family were known by sight on the island, and probably held in some awe.

A table tucked away behind an iron grille and up two steps successfully gave them privacy, which was what Stefan evidently wanted when he lunched out. The walls were painted white, as almost everything seemed to be in this sunny country, and small arched windows gave a view outside of fig trees and an apple tree with beyond that more house roofs and the distant rise of tree-covered hills.

Catherine left the choosing of their meal to Stefan, a decision he viewed with favour, since he only offered her the opportunity to choose her own with obvious reluctance. When the waiter had departed she looked across at him and tilted her head curiously.

'A *mezé*,' he told her in response to her question of what they were to eat. 'Do you know what that is?'

She shook her head, and his smile aroused her suspicions. 'Stefan, you haven't ordered anything I won't like, have you?' she asked, and he raised a brow as he poured wine from the carafe hastily brought by the proprietor.

'From what I have seen at home,' he said with a slow smile that dared her to deny it, 'there is very little that you do not like, Catherine.'

The 'at home' gave her a curious sense of security, but she felt a swift flush of colour in her cheeks to think that he had noticed her healthy appetite, and she looked down at her hands on the table. 'I know I shouldn't eat so much,' she told him. 'But it's all so – so gorgeous and I just can't resist trying it all. There's always so much of it too!'

For several seconds his eyes dwelt on the upper part of her body above the edge of the table, then he smiled, that same slow, blood-stirring smile. 'I do not think you have to be careful what you eat, do you?' he asked softly. 'I have seen no deterioration so far.'

It was disturbing to have him study her so clinically and Catherine felt her hands curling again into her palms as they often did when he affected her senses. 'I've – I've never had to worry about dieting, fortunately,' she told him with a laugh that sounded far too nervous. 'I suppose I'm lucky.'

'You are very fortunate indeed,' Stefan told her solemnly, the black eyes still watching her over the edge of his wine glass. 'You are a very beautiful girl, Catherine.'

'Thank you.' There was so little else she could think of to say. It was unthinkable that she should giggle like a schoolgirl, or dismiss the compliment as flattery, for Stefan would have scorned both reactions. Her quiet acceptance he would understand.

'You are dangerously so, I think,' he went on, and Catherine looked up at him swiftly, her eyes questioning his meaning.

'Stefan, I—'

He raised one large hand to silence her and twirled the stem of his glass between thumb and forefinger as he spoke. 'You must know that Nikolas finds you attractive,' he said, so coolly quiet that the conversation might never have gone from lighthearted comment on her appetite to something more serious, for all the change of tone he showed.

For a moment she said nothing, but her heart was hammering wildly at her ribs and she wondered, almost feared what was coming next. If he should tell her that she was a threat to his plans for Nikolas and must leave the island she did not think she could accept it as easily now as she would have done several weeks ago.

'I – I try to discourage him, especially when Miss – when Athene Pedopolous is there,' she told him. 'I don't know what else I can do, Stefan.'

He was silent for a moment, one long finger running around the rim of his glass and making a soft, squeaking sound that set her teeth on edge. 'Perhaps there is something I can do,' he said quietly.

Catherine blinked for a moment, looking at him with eyes that were both curious and wary, and wondering why he was behaving so out of character as to avoid looking at her. 'I don't understand you,' she said at last, and he smiled, a small tight smile that barely touched his wide mouth but brought a glowing warmth to his black eyes when at last he did look at her.

'You will,' he said softly. 'You will, little one.' He looked across at the approaching waiter, laden with trays. 'For now, enjoy your *mezé*.'

'What,' Catherine asked, willingly enough to drop the subject, 'is a *mezé*?'

'A four-course meal which you will have no difficulty in doing justice to,' Stefan told her, and his dark face lit with laughter when she saw the dishes and dishes of food being put in front of them.

Several cheeses, a relish of highly spiced cod's roe and the familiar stuffed vine leaves were some of the dishes offered as a first course, then followed various meat courses, including one of her favourites, *patcha*, which was lamb stewed with lemon and garlic and pungently delicious. The third course offered *kebabs* or as Stefan called them in Greek, *souvlaki*, and by the time Catherine had sampled those she was obliged to bypass the several delicious sweets offered and settle for a simple fresh fruit finale. Never in her life had she eaten such an enormous meal and the whole had been washed down by plenty of a fine white wine locally made and known as *Aphrodite*.

'I feel thoroughly ashamed of myself!' she told Stefan, and laughed softly when he shook his head.

'Why should you?' he asked. 'Did you not enjoy it?'

'It was wonderful,' Catherine smiled, then put a hand to her forehead and laughed again. 'But I think I've had just a *little* too much of that – what was it you called it?'

'The wine?' He smiled and the effect as usual, was devastating. '*Aphrodite*, you did not find it suitable for your taste?'

'I enjoyed it, like everything else,' Catherine assured him.

'And you do not like coffee.' He did not ask, but made it a statement of fact, and Catherine wondered at his having noticed her refusal of the Turkish brew his own table offered.

'I like some coffee,' she told him with a smile. 'But I don't seem to be able to take to the Greek variety.'

'I have noticed!'

Catherine looked at him through the thickness of her lashes, that insistent imp of mischief prompting her again, as it had done in the past. The urge to tease him even when she knew it would probably put an end to their present truce.

'Do you notice everything?' she asked with a smile.

For a moment he said nothing, but raised his glass to his lips and studied her over the rim of it while he drank, his black eyes deep and unfathomable. 'I notice most things,' he agreed softly as he put down his glass. 'And you have a gift for attracting the eye, Catherine. You have sat at my table for more than a month now, how could I not notice what you do, what you like and dislike?'

'I – I suppose not.' She felt her heart hammering at her ribs and wished, too late, that she had not been so rash. It seemed to her that he had something on his mind, but that he was still deciding whether or not to speak of it, and she had an uneasy feeling that it might concern herself and Nikolas. He had mentioned the matter once and let it drop because their meal was about to be served – she had no desire to have it raised again.

'Where do we go next?' she asked, taking a drink from her own glass, and Stefan shook his head.

'I would suggest that we go to the coast and seek the cooler air,' he said, 'but we have to drive out to see a friend of mine about those ponies for Alexander and Paul. The consolation is that it will be much cooler in the mountains than it is here.'

Catherine inclined her head, a smile glinting in her green eyes, ready to go anywhere with him in her present mood, and only vaguely aware that she was almost alarmingly light-headed from the effects of the wine she had drunk. 'Your wish is my command!' she told Stefan, and he smiled, a dark, unfathomable smile that lent a glitter to the black gaze that clung to her mouth.

'Not yet, *mikros eros*,' he said softly. 'Not yet!'

CHAPTER EIGHT

It was just like entering another world as they drove up into the mountains, and Catherine once again found herself enjoying it all immensely. The bright hot sun, the rocky, three-clad landscape all had a dazzling and challenging look that stirred her blood excitingly. Nor did she lay all the blame for her head-spinning lightheartedness entirely at the door of that vintage wine she had drunk.

However much wine Stefan had drunk with his meal, it had had no adverse effect on his driving, and she watched, as she always did, fascinated by the easy, confident way he drove the big car round and round the steep mountain roads.

The road was walled in places, with yellow-white

stone cut from the hills themselves, and overhung with a profusion of green, shaded here and there by trees. The surface was stony and dry and sent up clouds of white dust as they went round sudden curves, or skirted great soaring rock faces to which trees clung precariously to life.

The higher they went the cooler it became, and Catherine closed her eyes in sheer bliss when a slight breeze soothed the damp heat from her forehead. Stefan had promised it would be cooler in the mountains and already it was proving true.

The villa they were in search of appeared perched high up on a hillside, with the road running below, and the sun-baked rock above. It was enclosed in its own little plot of green, with fig trees, oranges and lemons and even the tall elegance of cypresses adding variety to shades of green.

The villa itself was white and built on staggered levels, square in outline, flat-roofed with its arched windows open to the air and its slatted shutters set wide in the usual way. It looked beautiful and not quite real in the brilliant white sunlight.

Surprisingly to Catherine, the owner was an Englishman called Alec Maine, and he greeted Stefan with an exuberance that spoke of long acquaintance, casting a surprised but appreciative eye over Catherine when Stefan introduced them.

'Granger,' he said, eyeing her speculatively. 'Would you be any relation to George Granger?'

'My father,' Catherine said, and glanced at Stefan as she said it, although she could not have said why.

'I met him a couple of times,' said Alec Maine. 'When he was about with—' The pleasant, friendly face showed acute embarrassment for a moment, and he turned to Stefan. 'Sorry, old man,' he said. 'I—'

'I am here to see those ponies I spoke to you about,' Stefan reminded him quietly, stemming an apology that could well have proved as embarrassing as his near slip.

There was no doubt in Catherine's mind that her father's companion on those occasions Alec Maine had mentioned was Helen Medopolis, and probably Stefan had no idea that she knew about that episode at all. It made her wonder if he would speak to her about it himself once they left the villa and what he would say when he knew that Nikolas had already enlightened her.

'Oh, yes, of course!' Alec Maine led the way round to the rear of the villa, glancing at Catherine as she walked between the two of them. 'Are you staying long in Greece, Miss Granger?'

It was a question that Catherine found surprisingly difficult to answer, and she instinctively glanced up at Stefan before she spoke. 'I – I'm not exactly sure,' she said, and would have made some attempt to explain her uncertainty if Stefan had not taken a hand.

'Catherine is staying with her brothers, Alec,' he said quietly. 'I am their guardian since their father died.'

'Oh, I see.'

No wonder the man looked startled, Catherine thought. Her pulses were racing out of control when Stefan's strong fingers curved about her arm in a disturbingly possessive way, drawing her close to the warm firmness of his body. Worded as he had worded it, his answer gave the impression that she too was under his guardianship, and she wondered if he realized how misleading he had been.

'You're not *my* guardian, Stefan,' she insisted quietly, and the fingers round her arm squeezed tight enough to hurt, as if to reprimand her for correcting him.

'I can think of no other suitable term,' he told her, and the black eyes looked down at her, glittering a challenge. 'What other word would you use, little one?'

It was just as if there was no one else there, Catherine thought wildly, conscious of Alec Maine's interested gaze. His challenge to her to deny that he was her guardian as well as the boys', those firm, possessive fingers grasping her arm, that oddly touching endearment, 'little one'. It was almost as if he was going out of his way to impress the other man with his authority over her, and automatically Catherine's independent spirit rebelled.

'I'd say I was a – a guest in your house,' she informed him, and her green eyes defied him to deny it.

Stefan shrugged his broad shoulders. 'Word it as you wish, Catherine,' he said coolly quiet. 'It does not alter the circumstances.'

In a country where mules and donkeys are prevalent, the sight of a group of sturdy little ponies in a shady paddock behind the villa delighted Catherine into exclaiming aloud. She even forgot her difference with Stefan when she saw them, for there was something so heartwarmingly familiar about the stocky, potbellied little animals in this strange land that she almost cried in a sudden surge of homesickness.

'The English families like them for the kids,' Alec Maine explained, perhaps understanding her reaction much better than Stefan could. 'They take to this terrain like ducks to water, I was quite surprised.'

'They're adorable,' Catherine said softly. 'They're – they're so English, somehow.'

Alec Maine smiled his understanding. 'They're Welsh, actually,' he told her. 'But I know what you mean. They're the ones you see hundreds of every Sunday, with assorted kids perched on 'em, clopping down country lanes, or trotting round somebody's meadow.'

For a few seconds they shared a moment of nostalgia, and then the encircling fingers squeezed her arm and brought Catherine back to reality, and she looked up at Stefan hastily. That he resented her sharing that moment with the other man was evident from the dark glint in his eyes and a small frown that drew his dark brows together, but his objection both puzzled and surprised her.

'If we may come back to business,' he said coolly, 'I would like to go into the paddock and look more closely at them, Alec.'

'Yes! Yes, of course!' Their host led the way through into the small, shady paddock, and Stefan turned as he went in and closed the gate behind him, leaving Catherine on the outside.

'I will not take long,' he told her. 'You will be better waiting for me out here, I think.' The black eyes held hers steadily for a moment. 'Too much nostalgia is unhealthily maudlin,' he added.

She had no time to object, but as she watched him stride, long-legged and arrogant, to where the ponies grazed it came to her with sudden and startling certainty that he was actually jealous of her few shared moments with Alec Maine. The knowledge so stunned her that for a long while she could only watch him from a distance, with her arms on the top rail of the fence, her chin on her forearms and a deep glow in her green eyes that made them shine like jewels.

It was two days before Nikolas found the opportunity to talk to her alone, and Catherine knew he was full of questions, from the way his dark eyes watched her during meals, or whenever she looked up and caught his eye.

She had been rather occupied for a couple of days with the boys. Ever since the arrival of their ponies they had been so full of enthusiasm for riding that there was no holding them back. They would have gone on all day, but it was Stefan who finally ordered a break in lessons, more for the sake of the two little animals than for his own or Catherine's benefit.

With Stefan leading Alex, she had been pressed into service as assistant teacher, leading Paul's pony by its rein while he did his best to follow his uncle's instructions. If they were to ride at all, they must learn properly, there would be no easy short-cuts with Stefan as their instructor, but they enjoyed it and so did Catherine.

Surprisingly Alex was proving the better pupil. Having more patience and quietness, his character lent itself more to learning and less to showing off as Paul was inclined to do. His uncle was pleased with his progress, and that gratified Alex as much as anything. There was, Catherine decided after two days in their joint company, quite a lot that was alike about Stefan and Alex, and the realization surprised her.

On one of the evenings since their trip to Cyprus, Athene Pedopolous and her father had come to dinner and the following evening Stefan had commandeered her for more than two hours, talking with her and his mother about Turkey, and about Madame Medopolis's early life in Greece.

Catherine had found the conversation enthralling and had been quite unaware of Nikolas's sulky dislike of the situation. She had discreetly refrained from mentioning the matter of the shares, and the misunderstanding that had arisen between her and Stefan about their disposal, although she had been tempted to speak of it. She thought from Stefan's expression once that he had expected her to as well.

'I have been unable to get near you,' Nikolas complained on the third evening. She had slipped out into the garden after dinner, and Nikolas had followed her. 'Stefan seems to go out of his way to keep you occupied.'

'I've been helping with the boys' riding lessons,' Catherine admitted, and wondered if that had been organized with the idea of keeping her from seeing Nikolas.

She remembered that when they were talking in the restaurant about Nikolas, Stefan had suggested he would do something himself about his brother's too persistent pursuit of her, since she had declared herself unable to do anything more to discourage him.

'Which he organized,' Nikolas said. His mouth showed that betraying hint of sulkiness again as he put an arm round her shoulders, and hugged her close to him. 'He seeks to part us, my lovely, but I will not allow it!'

'Nikolas—' She hesitated. Perhaps she should have shrugged that encircling arm from her shoulders, but it seemed such an unnecessarily brusque thing to do. 'Nikolas, I don't think you should – well, behave as you do with me. Not when you're engaged to Athene.'

'Has Stefan been talking to you too?' he demanded, and Catherine looked up at him, momentarily startled.

'He's – he's spoken to you about it?' she asked, and he nodded.

His good-looking face showed resentment and defiance and Catherine wondered at his having followed her out here when his brother had warned him about his behaviour. 'I knew he must have said something to you too,' he said. 'Because you have been avoiding me.'

'It was mentioned when we were having lunch the other day in Nicosia,' she admitted, 'but I haven't been avoiding you, Nikolas. Only Stefan's right, you know, you shouldn't be so—' Her shoulders shrugged lightly under his arm. 'You *are* engaged to Athene, after all, whether it was your idea or not, and you must be fair to her.'

'Fair to her!' Nikolas said bitterly. 'If it means I must lose you, Katerina? I will not!'

'Then you should have the courage to break off the engagement,' Catherine insisted, realizing too late how rash that could prove to be. If Nikolas did break off his engagement to Athene Pedopolous, Stefan would never forgive her.

'I cannot do that, Katerina,' he said. 'It would not be honourable!'

'Honourable?' Catherine stared at him for a moment, trying to understand the logic of his thinking. 'I don't see that it would be any less honourable than flirting with me while you're engaged to Athene!'

'You do not understand,' Nikolas told her with a sigh that should have evoked sympathy but only served to make Catherine impatient with him. 'Anyway,' he added, 'what good would it be when Stefan also has plans for *you*?'

Catherine shook her head slowly, staring at him in silence for several moments. 'Plans for – for me?' She was not sure whether to believe him or not. All the time she had spent with Stefan in the past two days he had said nothing about any plans for her and she would rapidly have put a stop to them if he had. He would know that well enough. 'Nikolas, you – you must be mistaken.'

'I am not mistaken,' Nikolas assured her, far less

appalled by the idea, obviously, than she was, despite his dislike of it. 'He told me that not only was I disgracing my family by behaving badly towards Athene, but that I had no right to behave as I do with you because he had other plans for you.'

'But he – he has no right!' Catherine protested huskily. 'He simply has no right, Nikolas!'

Her legs felt as if they had turned to water suddenly and her whole body was trembling. Somewhere in the region of her heart was a cold, heavy sensation that made her feel like crying, and when Nikolas bent his head and kissed her cheek she turned to him suddenly and buried her head against his chest, her eyes closed and her hands in tight little fists against his snowy white shirt.

He put his arms around her, startled she thought by her impulsive move, and held her close for a moment or two with his chin resting on her red hair. 'Nikolas – Nikolas, don't let him—'

'Nikolas!'

The voice was cold, stern and unmistakable, and Catherine closed her eyes again, her hands clinging tightly to Nikolas. When he was angry Stefan was dismayingly hard to out-face at any time, but now, feeling as she was, she knew she would simply break down and cry. He would think her a fool for crying and no doubt despise her for being found in such a compromising position with his brother.

Gently Nikolas disengaged her fingers and held her hands in his for a moment before pushing them away. He looked down at her, his dark eyes pleading for understanding, but he would do as Stefan wanted him to, she knew that without a doubt, and for a second she hated him for deserting her, as he inevitably would.

'I wish to speak to Catherine alone,' Stefan told him, and Nikolas took it as his dismissal.

'Nikolas!' She put out a hand to him in appeal, but he merely shook his head slowly and walked away, while Catherine watched him disappear into the shadowy trees with a sinking heart.

'So, you do your best to discourage him, do you?' The softly spoken words ran like ice water over her body, and she shivered. He was bound to misinterpret her appeal to Nikolas, of course, she should have expected it, and she could not face trying to explain to him how wrong he was. She did not turn and look at him, but made as if to follow Nikolas back to the house. 'Wait!' The order was harsh and peremptory. 'I want to talk to you!'

'I *don't* want to talk to you!' The tears were in her eyes, blinding her to everything but the last sight of Nikolas as he left her. Tears of anger as well as some other emotion that she could not yet recognize.

'Wait!' His strong fingers clamped about her wrist and successfully stopped her flight.

'Let me go, Stefan! Let me go!' There was an edge of panic in her voice and she tried her best to wrench herself free, struggling wildly and prising in vain at his fingers.

He swore softly to himself in Greek and tugged at the arm he held, bringing her round, breathless and still struggling against the unyielding hardness of his body.

Taking her other wrist and holding her firmly, he looked down at her, his black eyes blazing with anger.

'Will you *listen* to me?' he demanded harshly. 'Nikolas will not come back for you, it is no use you thinking he will!'

Catherine raised glistening, tear-filled eyes to that implacable face and shook back her hair in an unconscious gesture of defiance. 'Because you've bullied him into doing exactly as you want him to do!' she said bitterly.

'That he does not!' Stefan denied shortly. 'Or he would not have been out here with you, but he knows that I am right, no matter how he resents it. He owes it to Athene and to his family to exercise more restraint in his attentions towards you!'

'I've tried to tell him that!'

His expression showed his doubt of that, and he gazed down at her for a moment with such scorn that she felt herself curling up inside. 'So you told me,' he said coldly. 'But I have just witnessed how much you try to dissuade him!'

'But you're wrong!' she denied, and looked up at him appealingly, then realized suddenly that she was doing just what she had sworn not to do. She would not give him any explanations – let him think what he liked. If he thought her such a promiscuous creature perhaps he would think again about making plans for her future.

His voice was cold and harsh and his fingers curled as tightly as ever around her wrists, holding her against him so that she could feel the taut strength of his body, feel the anger that made him hard and unyielding. 'I was not wrong when I saw you in Nikolas's arms just now,' he told her bluntly. 'And you appealed to him not to go, you wanted him to stay – you cannot deny any of it, Catherine, I saw you!'

'You put the wrong construction on what you saw!' She no longer fought the steely hold on her wrists, but looked up at him with bright, glistening eyes, her palms pressed together like a prayer. 'You won't believe it, Stefan, because you don't want to, but it – it wasn't the kind of scene you thought it was.'

Very slightly the fingers around her wrists eased, but she made no attempt to withdraw her hands. 'Then perhaps you will tell me what kind of a scene it was that I witnessed,' he said, coolly quiet.

Catherine looked down at her hands, faced now with the prospect of telling him she knew of his plans for her. Of arousing that fierce anger again because Nikolas had spoken out of turn and warned her. 'It wasn't what you thought it was,' she said in a small husky voice. 'Believe me, Stefan.'

'I will believe you when you tell me why you were in his arms when I found you,' Stefan declared relentlessly. 'If you do not I shall be forced to believe the evidence of my own eyes.'

'You sound as if you have every right to decide what we do!' she cried, angry again because he was so adamant. 'You don't have the right to live other people's lives for them! You can organize Gregori and Helen into marriage, and Nikolas and Athene too, if he hasn't

151

the – the courage to tell you where you get off, but you're not making any arrangements for *my* future, Stefan! I refuse to be married off like some – some bartered bride! When I marry *I'll* choose the man, and I don't care whether anyone else approves of him or not – including you!'

His laughter stunned her completely and she stared at him in disbelief. 'So that is what is troubling you!' The black eyes glittered at her in the pale light of the half moon, and for one wild moment Catherine felt like hitting out at him. Her tears, her anger meant nothing to him, he simply found it amusing.

'I don't find the idea funny at all, Stefan!' she said, her hands clenched as she wrenched herself free of his hold at last and stood glaring at him. Her whole body was trembling with a chaos of emotions that she could not understand and all she could think of was the fact that he found the idea of her being married off to someone of his choice amusing.

He was serious again in a moment. His laughter was a rare thing and she regretted all the more that it had been directed at her. 'So Nikolas has been – indiscreet, has he?' he asked softly, and the black eyes regarded her for a long moment in silence, glowing like coals in the soft light. 'But he did not tell you who it was I had in mind for you, eh, little one?'

Catherine shook her head firmly. 'It doesn't matter who he is,' she told him. 'I refuse to marry anyone except someone I love!'

'And do you love Nikolas?'

The question was put so softly that she took a

moment or two to take it in, then she looked at him through the thick screen of her lashes. 'Would it make any difference if I did?' she asked quietly.

He smiled, a slow, meaningful smile that had the inevitable effect on her senses so that she curled her hands into her palms and avoided the steady gaze of his eyes. 'None at all,' he assured her quietly. 'But I would not like to see you hurt, Catherine.'

'You—' She sought for words to express the anger that kindled in her again. 'You're the most — cold, inhuman man I've ever met! You don't have a sensitive bone in your body, do you? All you can do is arrange people's lives to suit you! You never *feel* anything for anybody!'

'Be quiet!'

He spoke softly, but the glitter in his eyes made them hard as steel and his dark, strong features looked cruel in the softness of the moonlight as he looked down at her. Catherine felt her hands, her whole body trembling, whether in anger or some other emotion she could not tell. She only knew that in that moment she hated him more than anything in the world and she wanted to tell him so.

'I *won't* be quiet!' she retorted, her hands clenched tightly. 'I'm not one of your family, and I don't have to do as you tell me! I'm not a child either to be told to shut up just because you don't like what I say!'

'Katerina!' He said a whole lot more in Greek, his face dark and angry while Catherine stared at him wide-eyed and suddenly half afraid of what she had aroused in him.

She was totally unprepared for the hands that reached out for her suddenly, and pulled her hard against him. So hard that she could feel the thudding beat of his heart under the hand she put, flat-palmed, against his chest. His arms drew her closer still, as if he took resistance for granted and would not be resisted, one hand taking a handful of her copper red hair and pulling back her head.

'Cold! Inhuman!' The words were spoken harshly, and so close to her mouth that his breath warmed her lips. 'You dare to judge me so!'

His mouth on hers was more cruelly hard than anything she ever dreamed of, and she fought for a moment in sheer panic against its savage demands. But then something in her seemed to respond, even to such a primitive attack, and she made a soft little moaning sound as she lifted her arms to encircle his neck, moulding her soft body to the hardness of his.

His lips moved from her mouth to the slender softness of her throat and she held his dark head between her hands while he kissed her neck and the smooth curve of her shoulder. For a long moment she closed her eyes and yielded to the many and almost frightening emotions he aroused in her, then suddenly, with almost the clarity of a spoken word, she remembered Elena Andreas.

No matter if no such firm arrangement existed as between Nikolas and Athene, she had seen the way his cousin looked at him that first evening, and both Maria and Helen had said . . .

'Stefan, no!' She drew back her hands and put them

against his chest, attempting to push him away. The dark glow she saw in his eyes when he raised his head sent a shiver through her whole body, but she looked at him steadily for as long as she could bear. 'You're – you're no better than Nikolas,' she said huskily, still seeking to break his hold on her.

He held her now by her upper arms, his fingers digging into her soft skin. 'What is it you *now* accuse me of?' he asked, and sounded surprisingly controlled despite the tautness of his body and his hands as he fought to control the passion that had possesssed him a moment since.

'Elena Andreas.' Catherine whispered the name, and flinched when she saw the swift, dark glitter that showed in his eyes.

'What are you trying to say?' He shook her lightly and looked at her down that hawklike, Turkish nose. 'What are you saying about Elena Andreas?'

'That – that you're – that it's possible you're going to marry her,' Catherine said breathlessly. She looked down at the brown throat where it emerged from the whiteness of his shirt collar and hastily dismissed all kinds of disturbing thoughts. 'Maria said so.'

'Maria.' He echoed his sister's name softly and shook his head. 'I cannot scold our dear Maria,' he said quietly. 'But she should not have told you such stories, Catherine.'

'Nor Helen either?' Catherine returned swiftly, and saw the way his mouth tightened suddenly.

'Helen is Gregori's concern,' he said shortly. 'And Elena Andreas is the concern of neither of you, but since you seem to have made it so, I will tell you that I am *not* betrothed to Elena, and nor have I ever been. Does that satisfy you?'

Catherine had seldom felt more small or vulnerable in her life, and she shook her head slowly to clear it of the new and heart-stirring thoughts that were running through her head. 'I – you don't have to satisfy me about anything, Stefan,' she said. 'I – I'm sorry I spoke about it.'

For a moment he said nothing, but the grip on her arms had eased and she could almost feel him relax as he turned away and walked off a pace, taking out and lighting a cigarette. In the flick of the lighter's flame she caught the hint of a smile and marvelled at his rapid powers of recovery from such a storm of emotion. He drew on the cigarette once or twice, then moved back beside her again, sliding one hand under her elbow and turning her towards the house.

The light, almost sensual touch of his fingers on her sensitive skin kindled again those strange and disturbing desires, and she shivered. It did not even occur to her, as she walked with him through the shadowy trees, to remember the reason for her anger with him, or to discover if what Nikolas said about his plans for her were true.

'I think we should return, Katerina *mou*,' he said softly. 'Or more tongues will gossip, hmm?'

CHAPTER NINE

SINCE that eventful evening two nights ago, when Stefan had found them in the garden together and been so fiercely and disturbingly angry with her, Catherine had done her best to avoid being alone with Nikolas. It was not easy, for as soon as Stefan was out of sight he made an attempt to corner her.

So far she had been successful in evading him, but today he had spotted her as she was leaving the house to go for a swim, and followed her. He had caught up with her along the road to the beach and persuaded her to drive down to the north end of the island, a favourite spot for swimming, and her silence and preoccupation did not seem to trouble him at all, even if he noticed it.

The boys were visiting Cyprus with Gregori and Helen and their two little girls, and she had been rather at a loose end, but she would rather not have had the complication of Nikolas's company, no matter if she did rather miss it.

He had not liked the idea of her spending all the morning with Stefan and the boys while they learned to groom and care for their ponies as well as ride them, and he looked at her suspiciously now when she smiled to herself at some amusing episode that stuck in her mind.

Nikolas would never understand such preoccupation

with, to him, unimportant things. Stefan's patience with the boys never failed to surprise Catherine and she found it the one endearing quality she had so far discovered in him. He was stern with them if they deliberately misbehaved, but he never bullied them or lost patience, and the boys quite plainly adored him.

They were, in fact, getting thoroughly spoiled with a surfeit of admiration, she realized. For even Helen made much of them, although Catherine had the uneasy feeling sometimes that she loved them for their father's sake. It was an idea that she preferred not to dwell on too much. Such doting did not suit Nikolas, however, and it occurred to Catherine that he had probably been the apple of his mother's eye until the advent of her grandsons.

It was natural enough, of course, for Nikolas to be curious about the events of two nights ago, but she had still not quite forgiven him for simply going back to the house and leaving her to his brother's mercy. Not that she had expected him to do anything else, but it would have done more for her pride if he had been prepared to speak up for her.

Her answer that Stefan had raised no specific subject except that of their being together did not satisfy Nikolas, and he said as much.

'If it was only to speak to you about that, then why did he wish to see you alone?' he demanded.

He stretched out beside her on the sand, his hands behind his head, his eyes closed behind their dark glasses. He looked stunningly attractive in white slacks and a pale blue shirt that showed up his smooth golden tan, but Catherine was reminded of the time before when they had come here to bathe and been discovered by Stefan.

She wished suddenly that she had been more strong-minded about accepting his invitation, but she was not very good at resisting Nikolas's form of persuasion. Sooner or later, she felt sure, Stefan would realize they were together and once again take it into his head to come and find them.

It was the idea of his coming that made her so uneasy, but there was very little she could do about it now. Seeing his brother retire to his study to work. Nikolas had set out with the intention of catching up with her along the road. There was little hope of her avoiding him on an island the size of Dakolis, once he had set his mind on finding her, and she had allowed herself to be persuaded.

'It wasn't that he had nothing to say to me,' Catherine said with a wry smile. 'Far from it, I'm afraid, but I think whatever it was he meant to speak to me about got lost somewhere along the way.'

Nikolas opened one eye and looked at her curiously for a moment before he spoke. 'Did you quarrel?' he asked, and Catherine nodded, reluctantly honest. She would much rather have changed the subject altogether than talk about that evening and she certainly had no intention of letting Nikolas know its outcome.

'I suppose you'd call it a quarrel,' she admitted. 'We both said some pretty harsh things, I'm afraid.'

'And yet you were not angry with one another when

you returned to the villa, I will swear it,' Nikolas told her, and raised the dark glasses from his eyes, gazing up at her thoughtfully. 'Did you then kiss and make up, Katerina?'

The jest was too near the truth to be easily acceptable and Catherine turned her head away, giving her attention to a handful of sand that trickled slowly through her fingers. 'We made it up,' she allowed quietly.

Nikolas leaned forward, thrusting his face close to hers. 'You did not *kiss* and make up?' he insisted, and Catherine frowned.

'Nikolas, it has absolutely nothing to do with you if—'

'Ah!' he said swiftly. 'So he *did* kiss you!' He laughed softly. 'You are a very disturbing woman, I think, my lovely Katerina, to make my brother forget himself enough to indulge in moonlight kisses like a young lover!'

'Nikolas, you're being quite silly about nothing at all!' she told him sharply. She tried to blame the warmth in her cheeks on the heat of the sun, but she doubted if Nikolas believed it, any more than she did herself.

'But no! It is not – nothing at all!' he denied laughingly. 'You do not understand, my lovely. Stefan is not a man to go for walks in the moonlight and simply *kiss* a beautiful girl, he is more the—' Eloquent shoulders added unmistakable meaning to his words. 'Seducer? Is that the word I seek, Katerina?' His dark eyes searched meaningly over her face and he smiled. 'You were fortunate to escape with only a kiss, my lovely!'

'I don't know what word you seek!' Catherine told him shortly. He was enjoying himself at her expense and she resented it. 'But whatever you think of your brother, I assure you that I'm not that easily seduced!'

Nikolas eyed her for a moment, his eyes glinting, his brown face smiling, teasing her. 'Did you quarrel about me?' he asked, anxious to be the topic of conversation again, and Catherine recognized his vanity with a small inward smile.

'Partly, I suppose, in the beginning,' she admitted, willing enough to change the subject. 'Mostly we quarrelled about his interfering in my life – telling me what to do and arranging things for me that he has no right to.'

That, at last, disturbed his self-satisfaction and a small frown drew his brows together. He took off his dark glasses and sat with his arms resting on his raised knees, the glasses swinging from one finger. 'I wish you had said nothing about that,' he told her, and Catherine looked at him unbelievingly. 'He would know that I told you.'

'He did,' she admitted. 'But surely you must have known I'd tackle Stefan with it the moment I saw him, Nikolas. You must have known I wouldn't let him get away with that!'

'I suppose I did,' Nikolas allowed grudgingly. He sat for a moment gloomily silent, then creased his brows suddenly and narrowed his eyes as he looked at her quizzically. 'But if he knew that I told you,' he said,

'Why has he not – how is it? – told me off, huh?' Another searching gaze swept her features. 'But of course you settled the matter amicably, yes?'

'Eventually.' She looked down at her hand again with its palm full of trickling sand and remembered something suddenly that made her frown curiously. 'He laughed when I mentioned it,' she said quietly, half to herself, and Nikolas looked unbelieving.

'Laughed? Why should he laugh about such a thing?'

'I don't know.' She considered for a moment. 'He just seemed to think it was funny because I was so indignant and he wanted to know if you'd told me who – who it was he had in mind for me.' She looked at him for a moment. 'You didn't tell me that, Nikolas, did you?' she said. 'Do you know?'

Nikolas shook his head, but there was a curiously speculative glint in his eyes and a smile on his good-looking face that made Catherine distinctly uneasy when she saw it. 'If I did not know that such a thing is unthinkable – if I did not know Stefan so well—' He laughed and shook his head.

'Nikolas?' Catherine looked at him with a frown, and again he laughed and shook his head.

'If I did not know that it was ridiculous to think of such a thing,' he said softly, 'I would think that he had himself in mind, my lovely!'

'Oh, Nikolas, don't be so idiotic!' She sounded far more angry than the remark warranted, but suddenly the very same idea crossed her own mind and set her senses spinning chaotically. Her whole being was shaking like a leaf at the very thought of it being even remotely possible, but Nikolas was laughing again and shaking his head.

'Of course it was only a joke, my lovely,' he assured her. 'Not for a moment is such a thing possible!'

'No – no, of course it isn't,' Catherine said quietly. 'It's completely out of the question that a man like Stefan would find me even remotely desirable as a bride.'

Nikolas was still smiling at the idea of it, resting on one elbow, his handsome brown face looking up at her, confident and smiling. 'Not for Stefan, perhaps,' he said softly. 'But I would find you very desirable as a bride.' He reached for her hand and raised it to his lips. 'You would make a very beautiful bride, Katerina.' His dark eyes glowed warmly as he looked up at her, and his voice had dropped to that lower register that made it deep and seductive. 'We would make a very handsome couple, you and I, Katerina, hey?'

Knowing he was no more serious about that than he ever was about anything, Catherine smiled wryly and shook her head. 'From what I've seen of the way you treat *your* prospective bride,' she told him lightly, 'that's an honour I'd have no hesitation in declining, thank you, Nikolas!' She felt strangely vulnerable after his facetious suggestion about Stefan, and she had no compunction about retaliating.

Nikolas laughed softly. 'Heartless creature!' He bared his excellent teeth in a mock snarl and leaned towards her. Before she realized his intent he had rolled over and pinned her down in the warm sand, as he had done once before, his mouth seeking hers, his hands pressing hard on her shoulders. 'For that you will pay, my lovely!'

'Nikolas, no!' Catherine struggled, a sudden sense of panic stirring in her as she tried to resist his crushing weight and the strong pressure of his hands. He laughed softly, his mouth warm and sensual when it found hers and effectively silenced her, but it had none of the fierce passion that had made her yield so willingly to Stefan and she was more unwilling than she had ever been for him to kiss her.

When he let her go at last, she did not smile up at him as she might once have done, but looked at him angrily, her green eyes bright and sparkling with unexpected resentment. 'Katerina!' Her reaction puzzled him, that was obvious, and he frowned for a moment as he looked down at her. 'Why are you so angry, Katerina?'

Catherine pushed him determinedly away with both hands and sat up again, shaking the sand from her hair. 'You know why I'm angry,' she told him shortly. 'You're engaged to Athene – we've been through all that!'

'And you know how I feel about Athene,' Nikolas reminded her with a hint of his sulky manner. He disliked being rejected and made no secret of it. 'I do not *feel* anything for her!'

'Then have the courage to say so, and break off your engagement before you break her heart!' Catherine retorted, and added more gently, 'She loves you very much, Nikolas, and you're going to make her very unhappy if you don't try and change.'

'Why should I try and change if the stupid creature loves me as I am?' Nikolas asked, and Catherine was forced to see a kind of brutal logic in the reasoning. 'Also I cannot change,' he announced flatly. He took one of her hands in his and kissed her fingers, his dark eyes looking at her searchingly. 'Not for anyone but you, my lovely Katerina. What would you do if I broke my engagement to Athene? Would *you* then marry me?'

Catherine felt her heart lurch crazily and her imagination was already seeing Stefan's reaction to anything as drastic as that. If she had said the wrong thing to Nikolas, given him the wrong impression, then she must do her best to undo the damage she had done. Not for one moment did she want him to take such a step for her sake, only for Athene's.

'Katerina?' He kissed her fingers again lightly, and his dark eyes quizzed her, waiting for an answer. 'Shall I break off my engagement to Athene?' It was difficult to know whether he was serious, or if he was only teasing her as he had about Stefan wanting her for his bride, but she could take no chances.

'No, of course you won't break it off on my account!' She pulled away her hand and bit her lip anxiously as she looked across at the gentle breaking waves and the shining blue sea only a few feet away. 'That's the last thing I want, Nikolas,' she told him quietly, and glanced at him briefly through her lashes. 'You know Stefan would never allow it.'

'Stefan!' His eyes glowed like coals in a fair imitation

of his brother's. 'Always we must please Stefan. Even you, my lovely – you were such a beautiful rebel when you came here, but now even you are frightened of what Stefan will say to you!'

'I'm not—' She started to deny it, but knew it would be untruthful to do so. 'It isn't exactly fear of him,' she said more quietly, after a moment. 'It's just that – that he always seems to be so sure about things. And in this case he doesn't want to see Athene hurt any more than I do, he said so.'

'And you believe him?'

Catherine nodded, quite sure of her answer. 'Yes, Nikolas, I do.'

'And you think I am heartless, huh?' He resented the idea, she could see that, but it was true, if she faced the facts squarely. Nikolas was charming and attractive and he could do wonderful things to her ego, but it was all done with one object in mind and she would be deluding herself to think otherwise.

'Not heartless, Nikolas,' she said after a moment. 'But if you *are* going on with the – the arrangements that've been made for you and Athene, then I think you ought to consider her feelings more than you do, that's all.'

'That is all!' Nikolas echoed shortly. 'You speak to me as if you are a teacher of school! You lecture me as Stefan does, and then you tell me that is all!'

'Nikolas, please! I – I didn't mean to lecture you, but I wish, for my sake as well as Athene's, that you'd be less—' She stopped there, a warm touch of colour in her cheeks, not looking at him but sifting handfuls of

166

silver-white sand through her fingers and wishing she had never agreed to drive out here with him.

It was so quiet and peaceful and beautiful, and Nikolas was far too much of a temptation. Not that she deluded herself that she was in love with him, it was nothing as deep or emotional as that, but she found him attractive, as any woman would, and at any moment now she sensed he was going to try and persuade her. To try and make her forget Athene, and Stefan's disapproval, and succumb to his undoubted charms. But it was not Athene's plain little face that was before her, it was Stefan's stern, unrelenting one, and she got to her feet, suddenly determined, brushing sand from her dress and from her bare brown legs and arms.

'I'm going back, Nikolas,' she told him quietly. 'And I'd rather you didn't follow me.'

In a moment he was on his feet and standing beside her, his brow black as thunder, his hands gripping her arms so tightly that she gasped in protest. 'You will not walk away from me, Katerina!' he said sharply. 'I do not know why it is that you want to treat me so, but I think my brother has something to do with it, huh? He has forbidden you to talk with me alone and you are afraid of defying him!' His dark eyes searched her face for an answer, unwilling to believe that he had been rejected for any other reason than that Stefan had forbidden her to see him. 'Katerina!' He drew her against him and kissed her forehead lightly, his lips and his voice seeking to persuade her, whispering her name again as he lifted her face to him. 'Katerina, my lovely!'

For a second only she looked up into Nikolas's good-looking features, then suddenly she was seeing another face so close to her own. A dark, hawkish face with strong, stern features, blazing black eyes and a mouth so fierce it seemed to draw every vestige of resistance from her. She shook her head suddenly and broke from Nikolas's arms, running without a backward glance across the white sand and into the trees, only vaguely remembering in which direction the road lay.

'Katerina!'

She heard Nikolas behind her, calling her back, startled by her sudden flight. She heard him coming through the thick-growing, lush vegetation, anxious, determined to find her, and she ran even more swiftly up the slight incline to the road. Why she had chosen to make such a sudden and dramatic escape from Nikolas's efforts at persuasion she could not have said at that moment, but it had something to do with that brief but startling image of Stefan – something she did not attempt to explain.

'Katerina!'

The sounds of Nikolas's progress came closer and she sped on, quite breathless now and with her red hair rumpled and untidy from the snags of impeding branches. Oleander, hibiscus and mimosa all appeared and disappeared in her path in a riot of scent and colour as she ducked and dodged through the bushes until at last she saw the road just ahead.

She ran from the shadows into the brightness of sunlight and was blinded for as long as it took two arms to snatch at her and pull her to a standstill. Breathing heavily, she could only shake her head, but it was only a second before she realized that it was not Nikolas who held her, but Stefan.

There were fine-drawn lines about his eyes and mouth and a deep look in his black eyes that sent a sudden shiver of fear through her and she instinctively put up a hand to touch his cheek lightly with her finger tips. 'Stefan,' she said in a husky, breathless whisper. 'Stefan, what's happened?'

'Where is Nikolas?' His voice had a flat, cold sound and he looked across as his brother emerged from the trees, his breathing heavily erratic and his eyes bright and angry.

'So that's it!' Nikolas said in a harsh, breathless voice before Stefan could speak. 'I should have known it, of course!'

Catherine shook her head, but she made no attempt to move from the arm that encircled her shoulders, the long fingers spread wide to cover the bare top of her arm. 'I need you,' Stefan told Nikolas in a cool, quiet voice that again sent shivers of apprehension along Catherine's spine. 'Do not argue, Nikolas,' he added firmly when Nikolas looked like doing just that. 'This is urgent and important.'

He made a brief, concise explanation in his own tongue while the three of them walked towards the parked cars, and Nikolas glanced briefly and anxiously at Catherine. That, combined with the sound of her own name and Stefan's manner, convinced her that something was badly amiss, and she looked up at Stefan's face.

He looked suddenly older and much more sad than she had ever seen him look. His expression, his voice, everything about him forewarned her that something was very, very wrong and she appealed to him as he saw her into his car, while Nikolas got into his own without another word.

'Stefan, please tell me!' She turned to him appealingly as he started the engine. 'What's happened?'

For a second he said nothing, and Catherine wondered if, after all, he was merely angry at finding her with Nikolas again. But then, as they drove away along the narrow twisting road back to the villa, he took one hand from the wheel and placed it gently and briefly on hers.

'I wish I had time to break it to you more gently, *eros mou*,' he said softly. 'But there is no time, I must get back and join the search.' He glanced at her again briefly and Catherine held her breath. 'You know that Gregori decided to take Helen and the children over in the boat?' She nodded, feeling her heart already thudding against her ribs. 'There was an accident, and the boat was broken up,' he went on in a flat quiet voice. 'They have found Gregori, Helen and Paul so far.'

Catherine turned to ice. Her hands felt stiff and cold and her head felt as if it would burst with the pounding in her brain. 'They're not—'

Stefan shook his head. 'Gregori took the worst of the impact and he was unconscious, Helen became unconscious when they lifted her from the water, but Paul is unhurt.'

Catherine closed her eyes and thanked heaven for Paul's safety. It was a second or two before she took in the full meaning of what he had said and realized that he had made no mention of Alex or the two little girls. She was fond of Sophia and Melina, but her thoughts were all with Alex. Alex with his quiet ways and his serious little face and—

'Oh no! No, Stefan, no!'

The plea burst from her in a sharp cry and again those strong fingers closed over hers, pressing firmly, trying to still her fear, and she knew, even in her agony, that he wanted to do so much more to comfort her. To hold her in his arms and let her hide her face against his chest while she wept for Alex, but he had to get back, as he said, and help in the search that was still going on.

While it was possible that the other three children were still alive every available man would be searching for them, and it occurred to her suddenly how Helen must be feeling. She had been so utterly selfish in her first reaction that she had overlooked the fact that both Helen's little daughters were also missing, and she looked at Stefan's stern, dark profile with a new tenderness. He must be profoundly affected too, for he loved all the children, and especially his own two charges.

'Stefan!' She reached out impulsively to cover the hand nearest her on the steering wheel, and noticed how taut and white-boned the brown fingers were as they skilfully took the car along the undulating road at speed. 'Stefan, I'm – I'm so sorry.'

Briefly he turned his head and looked at her. 'Why do you apologize to me, little one?' he asked softly, and Catherine shook her head. His gentleness only made her more prone to cry and she did not want to make things worse for him by weeping.

'For being selfish,' she told him huskily. 'I – I could only think about Alex, but Helen—' She swallowed hard as she looked at him anxiously. 'How badly are Gregori and Helen hurt?'

'Helen had recovered consciousness when we heard,' he said. 'And Gregori was coming round. It was only then that it was realized there were three more children. They must have drifted away, perhaps on some of the wreckage.'

He was refusing to even think that they could have been drowned and she felt suddenly that she knew him so much better than before. She felt warmly and intimately close to him in a way she never had before and as he turned the car into the last approach to the villa, he turned his head again and looked at her. 'There *is* hope, Katerina,' he said softly, and even at a time like this, she noticed how pretty her Greek name sounded when he used it.

'They – they think the children may be found?' She dared not mention Alex, for the thought of him being out there somewhere in the sea did not bear thinking about, and she wanted so much to cry.

'There is a chance,' Stefan said quietly. 'I will not believe there is not. Everyone is searching, of course, but three such little ones—' He braked the big car to a halt and for just a second he bowed his head on to his arms, his hands gripping the steering wheel tightly, his deep voice whispering a short, fervent prayer in his own tongue.

The tears glistened in Catherine's eyes and she wanted to reach out and touch his bowed head, but before she had the courage to do so, he lifted his head and got out of the car. She did not wait for him to open the door for her but got out and stood on the broad sweep of the driveway in front of the villa, looking at him appealingly.

'What can I do?' she asked. Her eyes were wide and vulnerable, and the pain and anxiety she felt for the three missing children showed starkly in their depths.

Stefan paused only to hold her two hands briefly in his, his voice low and not quite steady. 'Pray for us, *eros mou*,' he said softly, and was gone.

CHAPTER TEN

THE house seemed so unnaturally quiet and Catherine shivered, though not with cold, for the sun was as bright as ever, although already sinking lower as the day wore on. She got up and moved across to the wide window and stood there for a while looking out at the now familiar scene. At the gardens lush and exotic with blossoms of every sort, the winding paths and the thick shrubs and trees that hid the stable where the ponies and Stefan's horses were kept.

She knew Madame Medopolis was watching her, and she felt the urgent need suddenly of someone to help her bear her unbearable sadness. She needed to cry, and she was not at all sure that Madame Medopolis with her serene façade hiding her grief would approve of her weeping as she felt like doing.

She half turned and looked across at the old lady seated on one of the ornate chairs, straight-backed and quiet, so calm in her grief that Catherine wanted to cry out to her. 'Katerina!' A small slim hand was extended to her, and Catherine went swiftly across the room to her, taking the hand in her own and seeing for the first time the deep and inconsolable sorrow in those black eyes that were so much like Stefan's.

Catherine sank to her knees and curled up beside the old lady's chair, her head on her lap. A gentle consoling hand was placed on her copper-red hair, stroking its glossy thickness back from her brow, enveloping her in the strange musky scent that Madame Medopolis always used, and the tears came.

'You want to weep, *cocuk*,' she said softly, the hypnotic movement of her fingers already having a soothing effect. 'Weep if you need to.'

'I'm – I'm such a coward about – things like this,' Catherine said, her voice muffled against a plum-coloured silk skirt that was infinitely soft against her cheek. 'I'm – I'm sorry, Madame Medopolis, I'm just not brave like you.'

'I am not brave, *bebek*,' Madame Medopolis told her kindly. 'I am older, that is all. I too weep for our little ones – Sophia and Melina as well as Alexander, but my tears are silent. You are young, you have the need to weep more honestly.'

Catherine closed her eyes, clutching the silken skirt and trying to shut out the recurrent vision of Alex out there in the sea, so small and frightened and so hard to see on the vastness of the ocean. 'Oh, *madame*, I can't bear it! I can't bear the thought of Alex – of Alex being—'

The gentle hand on her head lifted her face and the usually sharp brown features looked so infinitely compassionate that the tears started again in Catherine's eyes. 'I think you can, *bebek*,' Madame Medopolis told her softly, and used her own soft white handkerchief to wipe away the tears. 'You have borne tragedy before, little one, and you can again if it is necessary, which I pray God it is not.'

'Stefan asked me to pray for him,' Catherine said, seeing again his black head bowed on to his arms.

'Then you must, Katerina.'

It occurred to Catherine suddenly how much sadness Madame Medopolis must have known in her life. Her husband had died at quite an early age, leaving her with five children to bring up alone, and then she had lost both her daughters when both were very young. The thought of losing three of her beloved grandchildren must be almost unbearable to her, but she could still spare the time to console Catherine.

'I – I loved Maria as much as I did my own mother,' she said softly, and half to herself, and Madame Medopolis nodded understanding.

'Maria was a beautiful daughter,' she said. 'I missed

her very much.'

'So did I.' Catherine's voice caught in her throat when she thought of Maria's son too losing his life far too young. 'Alex is so much like her,' she said in a small tight voice. 'It – it somehow makes it so much worse.'

'Katerina!' Again the gentle hand consoled her, and she wept for a long time with her head bowed on the old lady's lap.

It was almost evening and the sun was almost gone when the telephone rang, and Catherine jumped up swiftly from beside Madame Medopolis's chair, her eyes wide and hopeful, red-rimmed with crying but hopeful at last. She stood for a long moment staring at the telephone and Madame Medopolis sat quite still in her chair as if she had been turned to stone.

Then a small thin hand gestured to the jangling instrument, a gesture almost of appeal. 'Please,' Madame said wearily. 'I have not the courage, Katerina.'

The statement startled Catherine, but she did not stop to query it, she darted across the room and picked up the receiver, her hand shaking as she placed it to her ear. 'Hello?'

The English gave her away, of course, and she felt herself draw a deep, sighing breath when she heard Stefan's voice at the other end of the line. 'Katerina!' He sounded so lighthearted, so relieved that she could not doubt what news he had and she felt the tears coursing down her face again, this time in sheer, blissful relief.

'Oh, Stefan!' Her voice choked in her throat, and

176

she turned swiftly to let Madame Medopolis see her smile. 'Mama is here,' she told him, blithely using the familiar title her family gave her. 'Oh, Stefan, we're so – we're so—'

'You can dry your tears, *eros mou*,' he told her, and she could so easily imagine that rare smile of his lighting up the dark strong features. 'They are all three of them safe. Bewildered, of course, and bruised and frightened, but they are safe!'

'I – I *can't* stop crying!' She was laughing and weeping at the same time, and if he had been near she would have kissed him without hesitation. In fact she wanted to do that more than anything at the moment, and she did not even question the reason for it.

Madame Medopolis came across the room towards her, and Catherine realized how old she looked suddenly, small and frail and still indomitable, but older than she had been a few hours since. Catherine handed her the receiver and she spoke to her son softly for several minutes, in Greek, then turned and smiled at Catherine, her head nodding slowly. She listened for a few seconds more, smiled at Catherine again then carefully replaced the receiver.

'Helen and Paul are coming home with Stefan,' she said. 'It is good news, Katerina, yes?'

'It's wonderful news!' Catherine said, her eyes bright with excitement. 'Oh, *madame,* I just can't believe it's all over!'

Madame Medopolis took her hands gently in hers, looking at her with those sharp but kindly black eyes, a small tilt to one corner of her mouth. 'I think now that

you have started, *cocuk*, you should call me Mama.'
The black eyes twinkled wickedly when she saw Catherine's blank look of realization. 'It will be appropriate, I think!'

Catherine did not stop to question her meaning, but was already listening for the sound of the plane returning, bringing Stefan back. She had, for the moment, forgotten that Nikolas, Helen and even Paul were with him.

It was another two days before Gregori was allowed to leave the hospital, but the day following the accident Stefan had flown Catherine over with him and they brought home Alex and the two little girls. Alex was very quiet at first, and inclined to cling to Catherine, but by evening Stefan had managed to persuade him to take an interest in his pony once again and, with his uncle and his brother's help and the natural resilience of children, he was soon back to normal.

Paul, with his customary buoyancy, seemed almost to have enjoyed the experience, and he chattered about it incessantly, given the opportunity, a fact that Nikolas viewed with exasperation. Although he had helped in the search for his nephew and two nieces he was no more attached to them than he had been previously, and Catherine, with her own love of children, was hard put to understand him.

Whether it was any of Stefan's doing or not, Catherine had no way of knowing, but Nikolas had made no effort to see her alone in the past two days and, while she felt relief that he had at last got the message, she was also curious to know what lay behind his sudden change. She suspected Stefan, but she could hardly ask either him or Nikolas outright, and so she remained in ignorance.

Her own relationship with Stefan had, in some way, undergone a subtle change. He was more gentle and less inclined to frown at her than he had been, and she felt much closer to him – the same feeling she had had when they drove back from the beach on the day of the accident.

It was hard for her to face, but she was forced to believe that his feelings for her probably went nowhere as deeply as hers did for him. The gentleness and compassion he had shown when he told her about Alex being missing had given her a new insight into his character and in some way had overwhelmed the resentment she had always used as a shield against finding him too attractive.

She found herself seeking ways of being with him, even though it was in the company of the boys, and only in the quiet of her own room did she allow herself to admit that she was in love with him. It was a hopeless kind of love, she knew, for she had admitted herself that she was not Stefan's idea of a bride.

One thing that pleased Catherine was the obvious change for the better in the relationship between Helen and Gregori. Ever since the accident they seemed to have grown much closer and she could only conclude that the worrying hours spent wondering if they would ever see their two little daughters again had worked the change. Helen had flown over each day to see Gregori in hospital and she had welcomed his return home with genuine affection and pleasure.

It was a relief to Catherine to see the change, for she had always felt terribly guilty about her father's part in Helen's unhappiness, and now it seemed Helen was appreciating her husband at last.

It was not Nikolas, but Stefan, who followed Catherine out into the garden one night, shortly after Gregori came home, and she had not been aware of his doing so until he spoke her name softly, just behind her. It startled her so much that she spun round swiftly, a hand to her throat and her eyes wide.

'I startled you?'

He had caught up with her as she reached the shadowy edge of the trees, and she was reminded of the first night she arrived on the island. As then, he leaned himself against one of the slim, plume-like cypresses and took out and lit a cigarette.

Then, as now, she had felt a strange stirring in her blood at the sight of him, only now she was much less overawed by him. Instead of eyeing him suspiciously as she had then she smiled, partly because, as on that night too, she wore a yellow dress. This one, though, was not simple and plain, but made of a soft clinging material that clung to her curves and floated about her feet and ankles.

She looked small and wraithlike in the pale lemon chiffon, at the edge of the dark trees, and Stefan watched her in silence for a moment. The light of an almost new moon did not penetrate the thickness of the trees so that she could see nothing of his face except the deep, dark glow of his eyes.

Her heart was tapping like a warning at her ribs, and she almost wished he had not come and found her. Clasping her hands close together to still them, she walked a little way into the shadows before turning to look at him again. Being more in darkness than he was she felt a little less vulnerable.

'Did you expect Nikolas?' he asked softly, and Catherine looked at him reproachfully, although it was doubtful if he realized it.

'No,' she said, steadying her voice with an effort. 'I suspect you've been talking to him again, and this time he's taken it to heart.'

'I would think he has,' Stefan agreed quietly.

She did not question his meaning, but turned again and walked on, through the bushes and trees, their colours dulled by the moonlight, but their scents heady and undimmed. Emerging again into the moonlight, she looked up at the sliver of yellow light, now only a pale shadow of the vast yellow globe it became in its prime.

Stefan had followed her, of course, she had expected him to, and her pulses made her disturbingly aware of him, as they always did. She did not look at him because it aroused in her all kinds of sensations she could not let herself feel. The proud dark head, those hawkish features with that arrogant nose and the mouth that smiled so seldom but could set her heart pounding when it did. There was so much about him that had become incredibly dear to her in the past few days and her heart ached to let him know how she felt.

Seeking a distraction from the disturbance of her own feelings, she caught sight of a small glittering object in the sand, almost at her feet, and bent to retrieve it, turning it in her hand for a moment before she identified it.

'It's from Helen's blue dress,' she said, and showed him a small silver bead. 'She lost it last night when she and Gregori came down here.'

'Then you can return it to her.'

He sounded very quiet and matter-of-fact, but Catherine's senses told her that he was no such thing, and her hand trembled as she curled her fingers over the shining bead. She laughed, a small, nervous little laugh. 'I've never known Helen and Gregori go for a moonlight walk before,' she ventured, wondering if he would object to having his family discussed so frankly.

He was walking only half a step behind her and she could feel the warmth of his body on her bare back and shoulders, feel the taut strength in the arm that brushed against her and sent a tingling along her spine that made her shiver.

'It surprises you?' he asked, and she shook her head, hastily bringing her mind back to Helen and Gregori.

'Not really,' she admitted. 'I've – I've just never seen them do such a thing since I've been here, that's all.'

'They love one another.'

The simple statement gave her a strange sense of pleasure, and she turned her head and looked at him over her shoulder, smiling. 'You speak with authority,' she said, and he nodded, apparently quite serious.

'I think I do.'

As on previous occasions his fingers slid beneath her arm, his palm warm and smooth and the fingers strong as they curled over her soft skin. Catherine's heart beat with such incredible force against her ribs that she felt quite breathless as she walked along the white beach, looking up at that sliver of yellow moon.

'You see,' Stefan said softly, close to her ear, 'how well my match-making can turn out?'

Catherine drew a sharp breath, turning to look up at him in shattering disbelief. She had been so deeply involved with her own feelings for him that she had forgotten his much discussed plans to find her a bride-groom, and she felt suddenly cold and stunned.

'You – you're not still trying to – to marry me off?' she whispered, her eyes searching his face which was maddeningly obscure in the faint light.

Only his eyes glowed down at her darkly and she could learn nothing from them. 'Do you not wish to be married?' he asked quietly.

'Not to—'

'Not even to a man you love?'

Catherine stared up at him. 'Oh, I *wish* I could see your face!' she cried in exasperation. 'I don't know if you're serious or not – I can't believe you are!'

'I am quite serious,' Stefan assured her.

'Then you're a brute! A cold-blooded, unfeeling, inhuman brute!'

'I do not like to be called such names,' he told her

coolly. 'And I would remind you, *eros mou,* that I have proved you wrong in that direction before!' He brought her to a halt and turned her to face him, his hands firm on her arms, only the thumbs moving caressingly on her soft skin. 'Do you not even want to know who it is I have chosen for you, little one?' he asked softly, and Catherine stared at him for a moment in silence.

'Not even to a man you love', he had said, and she had not noticed at the time; now she looked at him curiously. 'I don't love Nikolas,' she said in a small husky voice, and saw the whiteness of his smile briefly.

'And I did not name Nikolas, Katerina!'

'Then who is—' She caught her breath. His face was close enough now for her to see something of his features, and the expression in his black eyes was enough to set her pulses racing wildly as she gazed up at him with wide, questioning eyes. 'Stefan?'

His arms drew her close to him, folding round her, strong and irresistible until she could feel the vibrant warmth of his body through the thinness of her dress. She put her hands on his chest, spread flat and seeking that steady strong beat under her palms.

The glittering black eyes had a glow that warmed her blood like wine, and she lifted her arms to put them round his neck. She felt neither restraint nor inhibition as she tipped back her head and closed her eyes, but only a deep, strong sense of the inevitable.

His mouth on hers had all the fierce, possessive excitement she remembered, and she felt her control slipping away as she responded to the urgent need for him that had plagued her for the past days. The strength of the hands that both caressed and demanded, the words that he murmured huskily in his own tongue against her ear, were all part of the magic and she surrendered to it without a second ~~thought~~.

'You *will* marry me?'

His eyes glowed at her in the faint light, and she realized even as she did it that he would not see her nodding her head. She looked up at him, her eyes shining like jewels, and put one finger to the firm straight line of his mouth. Her heart was so light she almost believed it had stopped.

'Are you asking me?' she said softly, and he pulled her close again and kissed her fiercely until she was breathless.

'You will not play games with me, *eros mou*! I want an answer – now!'

'And I want to know first *why* you want to marry me!' Catherine told him. She was taking a chance, she realized, and almost laughed her relief when he crushed her so hard against him that she gasped.

'Because I love you!' he declared firmly. 'And I should make you sorry for the way you are behaving! Have you no pity, that you keep me in suspense like this?'

'Stefan!' She put up a hand to his face, her fingers soft against the rugged contours of his cheek. 'I wanted to hear you say it,' she explained softly. 'You see – you see, Nikolas said—'

'Nikolas has no doubt said many things he would have

been wiser not to!' he interrupted shortly. 'But I can imagine what it is that worries you.' He cradled her face in his hands and gazed down at her small face with its huge green eyes and smiled, one of his rare smiles. 'Will you believe me, my little one, when I tell you that I have seen no other woman since you came here? Will you believe me?'

'I believe you,' Catherine said softly. 'And I love you too much to let anything in the past deter me.'

'I would have asked you to marry me that night when I came out here to find you with Nikolas,' he said. 'But you were much too angry with me and you would not have believed my reasons then, would you, *eros mou*?'

'Probably not,' Catherine admitted, and sighed for the time that had been wasted. 'But I wish you'd asked me,' she added, with a small secret smile. 'You could have persuaded me to do anything once you'd kissed me.'

His arms were round her again, holding her to the hard urgency of his body, and he bent his head until his mouth was just touching hers, his breath warm on her lips. 'I must remember that when you are being stubborn again,' he told her. 'Now give me an answer at once, whether you will marry me! Or must I use persuasion to make you answer?

'I hope you will,' Catherine whispered softly, and had time only for a short, soft laugh before his mouth silenced her with an act of persuasion she could never resist.

Mills & Boon Classics

The very best of Mills & Boon
romances, brought back for those of you
who missed reading them when they
were first published.

There are three other Classics for you to collect this
January

FAMILIAR STRANGER
by Lilian Peake

Adrienne was determined to marry her fiancé, Clifford
Denning — but was 'determination' the right attitude to
take to something as important as marriage? Clifford's
brother Murray kept warning her that she was heading for
disaster but why should she listen to that overbearing
Murray?

BRIDE'S DILEMMA
by Violet Winspear

Tina married John Trecarrel in haste — and had time to
repent when she found out that she had to compete with
the memory of his beautiful first wife and that he was
attracted to Joanna's equally beautiful cousin Paula.

WITCHSTONE
by Anne Mather

When Ashley's father died she travelled northwards to live
with her uncle and aunt in their hotel. There she met Jake,
to whom she was attracted, but who had to be remote for
many reasons . . . most of all because of his forthcoming
marriage to Barbara.

If you have difficulty in obtaining any of these books through
your local paperback retailer, write to:

Mills & Boon Reader Service
P.O. Box 236, Thornton Road, Croydon, Surrey, CR9 3RU.

Mills & Boon Classics

The very best of Mills & Boon
romances, brought back for those of you
who missed reading them when they
were first published.

In
February
we bring back the following four
great romantic titles.

IF DREAMS CAME TRUE
by Roberta Leigh

Briony loved Christopher Clayton, but it was his brother she
married — a marriage of convenience to suit his ambition and
her financial needs. Would her career as a dancer be enough
to make up for the complete lack of love in her life?

BELOVED ENEMY
by Mary Wibberley

Holly Templeton hated Gareth Nicholas at first sight — a
situation that often leads to love at second sight! But there
was one good reason why that should not happen as far as
Holly and Gareth were concerned.

PALACE OF THE HAWK
by Margaret Rome

It was with typical ruthlessness that the arrogant Tareq Hawke
forced Lucille into becoming betrothed and then into getting
married to him. But would Lucille ever learn to care for the
domineering man who was her husband?

FEAST OF SARA
by Anne Weale

Set in the Camargue region of France, this story tells of a
young English girl who showed herself equal to the harsh
demands of life on a French farm — and to the proud spirit
of a Frenchman whom she had disliked at first sight.

If you have difficulty in obtaining any of these books through
your local paperback retailer, write to:

Mills & Boon Reader Service
P.O. Box 236, Thornton Road, Croydon, Surrey, CR9 3RU

A new idea in romance for Mothers Day

Mothers Day is Sunday March 29th. This year, for the first time ever, there's a special Mills & Boon Mothers Day Gift Pack* Best Seller Romances by favourite authors are presented in this attractive gift pack. The pack costs no more than if you buy the four romances individually.

It is a lovely gift idea for Mothers Day. Every mother enjoys romance in reading.

DANGEROUS MASQUERADE
Janet Dailey

TO BUY A BRIDE
Roberta Leigh

BEWARE THE BEAST
Anne Mather

THE CHILD OF JUDAS
Violet Winspear

*Available in UK from Feb. 13th

£3.00

The rose of romance
Mills & Boon

Masquerade
Historical Romances

Intrigue excitement romance

LYSANDER'S LADY
by Patricia Ormsby

The Polite World looked askance at Miss Katherine Honeywell, despite her beauty and fortune, when she insisted upon championing a social outcast. How unfortunate that she should have fallen in love with that arbiter of good taste, Mr Lysander Derwent!

CASTLE OF THE MIST
by Valentina Luellen

After her scandalous marriage to an impotent, elderly roué — undertaken to pay her brother's gambling debts — Isabel de Riché returned to Scotland with her reputation in shreds. And James MacLeod evidently believed every word ...

Look out for these titles in your local paperback shop from 9th January 1981

Doctor Nurse Romances

Don't miss
January's
other story of love and romance amid the pressure
and emotion of medical life.

THE GEMEL RING
by Betty Neels

Charity disliked and despised Everard van Tijlen, the
eminent Dutch surgeon whose fees were so
outrageously expensive. Then she found herself working
with him — and her ideas began to change!

Order your copy today from your local paperback retailer.